The
Mystery Fancier

Volume 5 Number 2
March/April 1981

The MYSTERY FANcier

Volume 5 Number 2
March/April, 1981

TABLE OF CONTENTS

WILDSIDE PRESS

Mysteriously Speaking ...

We have lost Bob Fish. He died on February 24 at the age of sixty-eight. Bob was a good writer. More importantly, he was one of the nicest men I have ever met. He will be missed.

In an effort to get back on schedule--this issue will go to the printer tomorrow, April 1 (no fooling)--I've thrown in virtually everything that I have on hand. The cupboard is now bare of articles, reviews, and, of course, letters. I managed to get this issue out within a month of the last issue, give or take a few days, and if I can do it again with the next issue TMF will be back on schedule for the first time in several years, and the May/June issue will come out at the first of May. To do it, I'll need your help, so send those articles, reviews, and l.o.c.s to me right away--I can't put out an issue until I have enough material to fill fifty pages.

There are a few new books that I need to mention.

Foul Play Press has recently reprinted, in quality paperback format, two of Stanley Ellin's novels: *Dreadful Summit,* first published in 1948; and *The Eighth Circle,* first published in 1958. They are priced at $4.95, which is high for paperbacks, but Foul Play has done a good job with them and they are worth it. Three more Ellin novels are scheduled for publication this summer: *The Key to Nicholas Street, The Panama Portrait,* and *The Winter After This Summer.*

The same publisher has issued three more Phoebe Atwood Taylor books with mystery celebrity covers, same as the Ellin books in quality and price. Joan Kahn is the featured victim on the cover of *Cold Steal*; Otto Penzler expires on the front of *The Six Iron Spiders*; and Michele Slung makes a lovely corpse for *Proof of the Pudding.* If you bought earlier books by Foul Play Press and were put off by the near-pulp paper, be advised that Foul Play has shaped up and is now using good, white paper.

In the wake of the recent Drood discussions in these pages comes a new conclusion by Leon Garfield. Published by Pantheon Books at $12.95, this handsome version of *The Mystery of Edwin Drood* has extensive period illustrations by Antony Maitland and an introduction by Edward Blishen. The first 204 pages are by Dickens, and Garfield's completion consumes another 123 pages.

I am advised that there are still available a few copies

SPY SERIES CHARACTERS IN HARDBACK, VII

By Barry Van Tilburg

DOSSIER #38: Marcus Farrow.
CREATED BY: Angus Ross.
OCCUPATION: Agent for super-secret department of British Intelligence referred to simply as the Section.
ASSOCIATES: The Chief, head of Section; Charlie McGowan, super clean, non-smoking, non-drinking, non-swearing fellow agent.
WEAPONS: Pistols, but prefers his hands whenever possible.
OTHER COMMENTS: Farrow is a down to earth person who prefers the simple things in life--food, drink, and travel. He lives in a caravan, and is always getting into violent situations. In one book his girl friend and his caravan are blown up by a bomb meant for him.
The Manchester Thing (Long, 1970).
The Huddersfield Job (Long, 1971).
The London Assignment (Long, 1972).
The Dunfermline Affair (Long, 1973).
The Bradford Business (Long, 1974).
The Amsterdam Diversion (Long, 1974).
The Leeds Fiasco (Long, 1975).
The Edinburgh Exercise (Long, 1975).
The Ampurias Exchange (Long, 1976; Walker, 1977).
The Aberdeen Conundrum (Long, 1977).
The Burgos Contract (Long, 1978).
The Congleton Lark (Long, 1979).
The Hamburg Switch (Long, 1980).

DOSSIER #39: George Mado.
CREATED BY: Warren Tute.
OCCUPATION: Agent for British Intelligence.
ASSOCIATES: Philip Tarnham, traitor; Elissa Tarnham, Philip's wife, who marries Greek millionaire Marides after Philip's death; Panayotis Marides, the millionaire; Ann Mado, George's wife.
WEAPONS: Pistols.
OTHER COMMENTS: Mado has been referred to as a hard-drinking, lecherous, burnt-out old agent. He has been captured, tortured, and blown. But British Intelligence uses him to divert attention from other matters. George, however, always draws too much attention for his own good.
A Matter of Diplomacy (Dent, 1969).
The Powder Train (Dent, 1970).
The Tarnham Connection (Dent, 1971).
The Resident (Constable, 1973).
Next Saturday in Milan (Constable, 1975).
The Cairo Sleeper (Constable, 1977).

---

of Dorothy L. Sayers' *Wilkie Collins: A Critical and Biographical Study*, edited from the manuscript by E.R. Gregory. This 120 page softbound book was published in 1977 in a limited edition of 1,000 copies and can be had by sending a check for $12.50 (overseas postage add $1.00) made payable to The Friends of the University of Toledo Libraries, 2801 W. Bancroft St., Toledo, Ohio 43606. I have not seen the book.

AN INDEX OF BOOKS REVIEWED IN TMF VOLUME FOUR
COMPILED BY DAVID H. DOERRER

3

Estleman, Loren D., MOTOR CITY BLUES (Fred Dueren)   4:46
Evans, John, HALO FOR SATAN (S. Lewis)   3:41
Flowers, Charles, IT NEVER RAINS IN LOS ANGELES (M. J.
   DeMarr)   1:30
Forbes, Stanton, THE WILL AND LAST TESTAMENT OF
   CONSTANCE COBBLE (S. Lewis)   3:37
Francis, Dick, WHIP HAND (S. Lewis)   4:37
Fredman, Mike, KISSES LEAVE NO FINGERPRINTS (S. Lewis)   5:32
_____, YOU CAN ALWAYS BLAME THE RAIN (S. Lewis)   4:36
Freeling, Nicholas, CASTANG'S CITY (Jane S. Bakerman)   5:40
_____, THE NIGHT LORDS (J. S. Bakerman)   2:42
Freemantle, Brian, CHARLIE M (T. P. Dukeshire)   2:50
_____, HERE COMES CHARLIE M (T. P. Dukeshire)   2:50
Garrity, Dave J., DRAGON HUNT (S. Lewis)   2:38
Gash, Jonathan, THE GRAIL TREE (S. Lewis)   5:34
Geller, Michael, A CORPSE FOR A CANDIDATE (S. Lewis)   3:39
Gibson, Walter B., THE SHADOW SCRAPBOOK (Mike Nevins)   2:51
Gilbert, Michael, THE KILLING OF KATIE STEELSTOCK
   (S. Lewis)   5:30
Gores, Joe, GONE, NO FORWARDING (M. Nevins)   2:51
Granger, Bill, PUBLIC MURDERS (S. Lewis)   3:35
Guthrie, A. B. Jr., NO SECOND WIND (S. Lewis)   3:36
Hale, Christopher, MURDER ON DISPLAY (S. Lewis)   3:40
Hale, Robert Lee, THE KING EDWARD PLOT (G. M. Townsend)   2:46
Hamilton, Donald, THE INTRIGUERS (M. M. Wooster)   3:46
Harris, Timothy, GOOD NIGHT AND GOOD-BYE (T.P. Dukeshire)   2:50
Hensley, Joe L., MINOR MURDERS (S. Lewis)   2:36
_____,   "   "   (F. M. Nevins, Jr.)   1:32
Higgins, George V., KENNEDY FOR THE DEFENSE (F. M.
   Nevins, Jr.)   5:43
Household, Geoffrey, THE COURTESY OF DEATH (M.M. Wooster)   3:45
Howes, Royce, THE CASE OF THE COPYHOOK KILLING (S. Lewis)   4:33
Jeffries, Roderick, MURDER BEGETS MURDER (S. Lewis)   2:32
Keating, H.R.F., THE MURDER OF THE MAHARAJAH (S. Lewis)   4:40
King, Stephen, NIGHT SHIFT (M. M. Wooster)   3:45
Kienzle, William X., DEATH WEARS A RED HAT (G.M.
   Townsend)   2:42
_____, THE ROSARY MURDERS (J.S. Bakerman)   2:41
Langton, Jane, THE MEMORIAL HALL MURDER (David McGee)   1:29
Laurance, Alice and Isaac Asimov, eds., WHO DONE IT?
   (F. M. Nevins, Jr.   4:48
Leather, Edwin, THE DUVEEN LETTER (S. Lewis)   5:33
_____, THE MOZART SCORE (Ellen Nehr)   1:34
Lewin, Michael Z., NIGHT COVER (S. Lewis)   4:39
_____, OUTSIDE IN (S. Lewis)   5:33
Lewis, Roy Harley, A CRACKLING OF SPINES (R.L. Wenstrup)   5:38
Lore, Phillips, THE LOOKING GLASS MURDERS (S. Lewis)   5:29
Lutz, John, JERICHO MAN (F. M. Nevins, Jr.)   5:37
McCloy, Helen, BURN THIS (S. Lewis)   4:42
McGivern, William P., REPRISAL (S. Lewis)   2:34
MacLean, Alistair, ATHABASCA (B. Crider)   5:40
MacLeod, Charlotte, THE LUCK RUNS OUT (J. S. Bakerman)   2:49
_____,   "   "   "   "   (E. Nehr)   1:34
_____, REST YOU MERRY (J. S. Bakerman)   2:48
_____, THE WITHDRAWING ROOM (J.S. Bakerman)   6:39
McMullen, Mary, A COUNTRY KIND OF DEATH (J.S. Bakerman)   2:46
_____, A DANGEROUS FUNERAL (J. S. Bakerman)   2:45
Maryk, Michael and Brent Monahan, DEATHBITE
   (G. M. Townsend)   2:43

Mason, A.E.W., MURDER AT THE VILLA ROSE (S. Lewis)   5:28
Olson, Donald, SLEEP BEFORE EVENING (S. Lewis)   2:35
Panek, LeRoy, WATTEAU'S SHEPHERDS: THE DETECTIVE NOVEL
  IN BRITAIN, 1914-1940 (F. M. Nevins, Jr.)   3:44
Parker, Robert B., LOOKING FOR RACHEL WALLACE (S. Lewis)   3:34
_____, WILDERNESS (S. Lewis)   2:33
Parrish, Frank, STING OF THE HONEYBEE (S. Lewis)   2:31
Patterson, Richard North, THE LASKO TANGENT (S. Lewis)   5:31
Peebles, Niles N., BLOOD BROTHER, BLOOD BROTHER
  (S. Lewis)   2:37
Pentecost, Hugh, BEWARE YOUNG LOVERS (S. Lewis)   3:40
Perowne, Barry, RAFFLES OF THE ALBANY: FOOTPRINTS OF A
  FAMOUS GENTLEMAN CROOK IN THE TIMES OF A GREAT
  DETECTIVE (M. M. Wooster)   3:44
Peters, Ellis, A MORBID TASTE FOR BONES (S. Lewis)   4:37
_____, ONE CORPSE TOO MANY (S. Lewis)   4:34
Phillips, David Atlee, THE CARLOS CONTRACT
  (T. P. Dukeshire)   2:50
Picano, Felice, THE LURE (F. Dueren)   4:46
Porter, Joyce, DEAD EASY FOR DOVER (G. M. Townsend)   1:31
Pronzini, Bill, LABYRINTH (S. Lewis)   3:38
_____,   "   (F. M. Nevins, Jr.)   3:43
Quentin, Patrick, PUZZLE FOR FIENDS (S. Lewis)   4:40
Reasoner, James M., TEXAS WIND (B. Crider)   6:38
Reilly, John M., ed., TWENTIETH CENTURY CRIME AND
  MYSTERY WRITERS (S. Lewis)   5:27
Rendell, Ruth, MEANS OF EVIL (S. Lewis)   2:34
Rhode, John, HENDON'S FIRST CASE (Paul McCarthy)   4:44
Riley, Dick and Pam McAllister, eds., THE BEDSIDE,
  BATHTUB & ARMCHAIR COMPANION TO AGATHA CHRISTIE
  (F. M. Nevins, Jr.)   1:33
Rilla, Wolf, THE CHINESE CONSORTIUM (S. Lewis)   5:34
Ross, Angus, THE HAMBURG SWITCH (F. Dueren)   4:46
Russell, Richard, PAPERBAG (S. Lewis)   2:32
Sanders, Lawrence, THE TENTH COMMANDMENT (B. Crider)   5:39
Schier, Norma, THE ANAGRAM DETECTIVES (Ansin F. Scremvin)1:32
Sladek, John, BLACK AURA (S. Lewis)   2:37
Snow, C.P., THE AFFAIR (J. L. Breen)   6:34
Swan, Phyllis, FIND SHERRI! (S. Lewis)   3:36
Taylor, John Russell, HITCH: THE LIFE AND TIMES OF
  ALFRED HITCHCOCK (M. Nevins)   2:52
Thorp, Roderick, NOTHING LASTS FOREVER (F.M. Nevins, Jr.)1:33
Tippette, Giles, WILSON'S GOLD (B. Crider)   3:43
Trevor, Bernard, BRIGHTLIGHT (Bob Adey)   3:42
Truman, Margaret, MURDER IN THE WHITE HOUSE
  (F. M. Nevins, Jr.)   4:47
Valin, Jonathan, THE LIME PIT (S. Lewis)   4:35
Watson, John H., M.D., as edited by Loren D. Estleman,
  DR. JEKYLL AND MR. HOLMES (S. Lewis)   2:34
Wells, Charlie, THE LAST KILL (T. P. Dukeshire)   1:30
Webster, Noah, AN INCIDENT IN ICELAND (S. Lewis)   2:32
White, Terence de Vere, MY NAME IS NORVAL (D. McGee)   1:29
Winn, Dilys, ed., MURDERESS INK: THE BETTER PART OF THE
  MYSTERY (E. Nehr)   1:35
Yorke, Margaret, THE COST OF SILENCE (J. S. Bakerman)   5:41
_____, DEAD IN THE MORNING (S. Lewis)   2:40
Zochert, Michael, ANOTHER WEEPING WOMAN (S. Lewis)   5:30

LACHMAN'S REVIEWS
IN TMF VOLUMES TWO THROUGH FOUR

COMPILED BY DAVID H. DOERRER

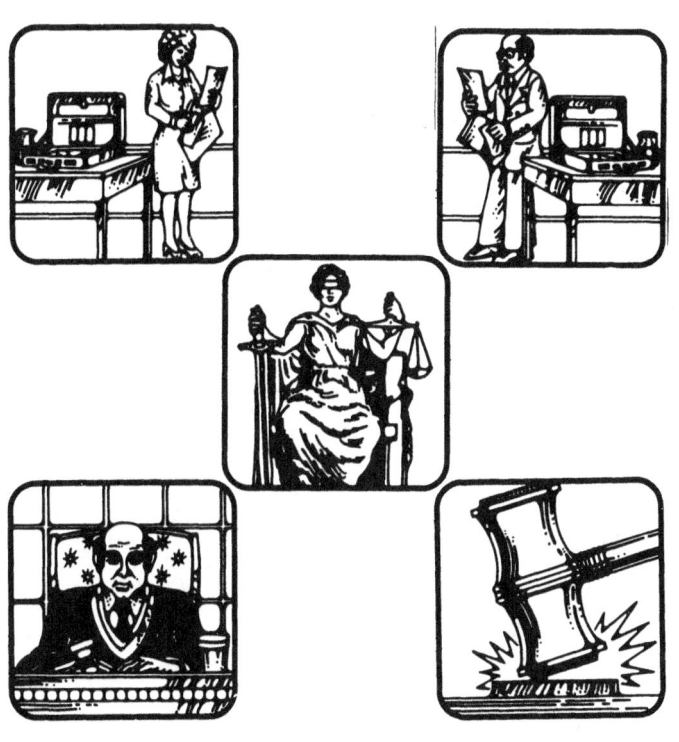

It's About Crime

By Marvin Lachman

NOTES ON RECENT READING

It's amazing how quickly a mystery can become dated. Jeffrey Hudson's *A Case of Need* was only published in 1968, and it was considered a very "with it" book about drugs, abortion, and murder. A doctor is charged with murder in a death resulting from an illegal abortion. Another doctor, who reminds me of Alan Alda in M*A*S*H, turns detective to try to prove his friend innocent. Shortly after 1968, abortions became legal almost everywhere, rendering this book analogous to a 1928 novel about rum-running.

Still, this is a good book and very authentic, since the author is really Michael Crichton, M.D., who practiced medicine until he hit it big with *The Andromeda Strain*. His pseudonym displays his sense of humor, since Jeffrey Hudson was the name of a dwarf in the court of Charles II; Crichton is six feet, nine inches tall. A bonus is in-jokes used by doctors, e.g., "Did you hear about the French biochemist who hat twins? He baptized one and kept the other as a control."

Too many writers have taken the mystery out of mysteries. Not only is the ending predictable, but it's easy to figure how the author will get there. Suspense and surprise are absent. A notable exception is Andrew Garve whose *The Lester Affair* (1974) is a good example of a different detective story. James Lester is the Progressive Party's candidate for British Prime Minister and the favorite in the election when an attractive girl makes allegations about him. She says they sun-bathed in the nude and made love aboard his yatch. His denial is blown up into a national issue. Unless he can prove he is telling the truth, he faces loss of the election and a conviction for perjury. It's all very plausible and fast-moving.

Readers of TMF, *The Poisoned Pen*, and DAPA-EM might guess that I don't like Private Eye novels because I have savaged so many of them in recent reviews. Quite the contrary. I grew up on Hammett and Chandler and then graduated to Gault, Dewey, Howard Browne, and Ross Macdonald (before he went into mimeo). That is why I am annoyed by the recent spate of mediocrity or worse in this sub-genre. One of the poorest is Kin Platt's *The Princess Stakes Murder* (Charter, $2.25). There is hardly an original word in this story of Max Roper's investigation into the murder of a famous jockey. What passes for

Roper's detection is a parody of that art. For example, he gets information by threatening to throw someone he is questioning out of a twenty-third-floor window. Karate is his specialty, and if there is anything more boring than written descriptions of nose-breaking blows and lectures on the method by which they are delivered, I haven't read it yet.

And talk about cliches, Plat uses them all, e.g.:

1. (Prior to Roper finding a dead body) "I knocked on the door and called her name. She didn't answer and I had that old, cold feeling and walked in."

2. (Roper is about to get crucial information from a man) "Something whistled, glittering in the night. It thudded heavily close to me.... He coughed and fell against me. I judged the knife in his back to have at least a six-inch blade."

3. (Roper gets slugged) "Rockets sputtered inside my head ... as I went down, all those sputtering rockets looping around inside my skull went out one by one. Darkness enveloped me, dragging me down and down until I couldn't fall any farther."

4. (Roper gets drugged) "The room spun and the iron band inside my head exploded into a battery of rockets. They all went off, one by one, followed by a cascade of brilliant lights."

5. (Roper's creator sees page 192 approaching) "I thought about everybody connected with Willie Rich who might have a particular reason for wanting him dead.... I thought it was about time I went for the killer."

I'm not sure why anyone who wants to read a horseracing mystery would read Kin Platt if Dick Franis is available. The latter's *Whip Hand* (1979) has just been reprinted by Pocket Books for $2.75. This is the second novel to feature Sid Halley, who first appeared in *Odds Against* and attracted many viewers to the TV version of that book on PBS's *Mystery* last year. Now a private detective specializing in racing cases, Halley is as brave and stoical as ever. The villains who face him are as evil as ever. Francis involves Halley in three crimes, two too many for maximum effectiveness. If not the very best Dick Francis, *Whip Hand* is very good indeed.

One of the best series in paperback is the Inspector Sloan books of Catherine Aird. The latest is *A Late Phoenix* (Bantam, $2.25). Aird is not only a talanted writer; she also is a scholar in the field, having written a biography of Josephine Tey. She does not write many novels, but she obviously tries to make each one somewhat special.

Taking a situation which in recent years has become hackneyed (the crime with roots far in the past), she breathes life into it. A skeleton has been discovered in the ruins of a World War II bomb site, and Sloan finds that many citizens in the British market town of Berebury are worried. Aird provides more than just a well-plotted, subtly-clued detective story, though that would have been enough. She also gives the reader a likeable, literate detective and the fascinating contrast between British life during the Battle of Britain and the early 1970's (the hardbound edition was published in 1971).

Often, in my reviews, I have bemoaned the lack of subtlety most current writers show in handling sex. In Evelyn Berckman's *A Case in Nullity* (1967), a crime novel about a nonconsumated marriage, it is handled *too* subtly. There is also an almost incredible lack of verbal communication between the husband and wife. Still, Berckman writes well, and the book makes vivid the vulnerability of decent people to the acts of a clever psychopath.

I haven't read Walter Wager's *Blue Leader* (Berkley, $2.25) yet, but I can review the cover. It's by Robert McGinnis, the first new cover by him I've seen in several years. The master is in good form with his portrait of sexy female Private Eye A.B. Gordon. Oh those eyes, etc....

MISCELLANEOUS MYSTERY MISH-MASH

Reading newspapers carefully, I am amazed at the number of mystery-related items I caom across. For those who may have missed them, I pass along the following:

1. The Albany, that stylish apartment building where A.J. Raffles hung his burglar tools, is still open and is considered one of London's best addresses.

2. Charles Goodrum is known for his mysteries with a library background. He recently published *Treasures of the Library of Congress* (Abrams, $50), a large, well-illustrated history of the building that I missed when I went to Washington for Bouchercon.

3. New Yorker Herbert Mitgang recently interviewed Ngaio Marsh by calling her in Christchurch, New Zealand. Inevitably, he used the line in his write-up: "There is nothing like a Dame." Among Miss Marsh's comments were: "I am in the line of the original detective story, where a crime is solved calmly. ... I don't read much detective fiction myself; that would be too much like a busman's holiday."

4. Someone in New York City had his or her heart in the right place by renaming part of West 84th Street to honor Poe. The only problem was that the sign they put up spelled it Edgar Allen Poe.

5. Sometimes scrutiny of the papers brings the bad news that a mystery writer has died. Late in 1980, Richard Ellington died in the U.S. Virgin Islands. He had written radio scripts for *The Shadow* and *The Fat Man*. He also published five novels about Private Eye Steve Drake between 1948 and 1953.

Robert L. Fish, a familiar visitor at most Bouchercons (and Guest of Honor in 1975), died on February 24, 1981, at the age of 68 in Trumbill, Connecticut. We all know about his mysteries. His obit disclosed that recently, in collaboration with the soccer star, he wrote the biography *Pelé: My Life and a Wonderful Game.*

Mystery * File

Short Reviews
By Steve Lewis

Francis L. and Roberta B. Fugate. *Secrets of the World's
   Best-Selling Writer*. Morrow, 1980, 286 pp., $12.95.
Erle Stanley Gardner. *The Human Zero: The Science Fiction
   Stories of Erle Stanley Gardner*. Edited by Martin H.
   Greenberg and Charles G. Waugh. Morrow, 1981, 444 pp.,
   $12.95.

   Erle Stanley Gardner often proudly referred to himself as
a fiction factory. The total sales of all the books he ever
wrote, in all languages and in all editions, is currently
estimated at well over 300 million copies. His isolated ranch
near Temecula, California, grew to include twenty-two build-
ings, designed to house himself, his secretarial staff, and
his voluminous, all-inclusive archives.
   All of his earliest writing was done for the "woodpulp"
magazines, those ephemeral pieces of popular culture disdained
at the time by librarians and the literary establishment alike.
The covers were lurid and garish; the contents were written to
match. If you were to find an attic filled with them today,
you would have a small fortune on your hands.
   By 1933, Erle Stanley Gardner was a household word. Series
characters such as Lester Leith, Speed Dash, Ed Jenkins, Senor
Lobo, Sidney Zoom, and scores of others were the lifeblood of
a list of pulp magazines a page long. In that year alone,
Gardner had a total of seventy short stories, novelettes, and
articles see print.
   It was also the year that Perry Mason came along. Morrow
published *The Case of the Velvet Claws* in March of that year,
and *The Case of the Sulky Girl* followed in quick order. In
1934 Gardner's production of short pieces fell off a bit, to
something just under forty or so, but to compensate there were
three more Mason novels.
   Perry Mason immediately captured the nation's attention.
Originally conceived as a hard-boiled attorney named Ed Stark,
straight from the pages of *Black Mask* magazine, which also
gave Dashiell Hammett and Raymond Chandler good running
starts on their careers, Mason went on to be the star perform-
er in a total of eighty-five novels.
   They were formula stuff, but Gardner knew exactly what his
readers wanted. Each of the cases culminated in a courtroom
scene, with a trial and the future of Mason's client hanging
in the balance. Gardner's own background as a practicing

attorney helped provide for some of the trickiest shenanigans
ever defised, most of it well beyond the reach, one imagines,
of even such superstars of the profession as F. Lee Bailey and
Louis Nizer, to name two.

There were also comic strips, a radio show, and, of course,
the long-running Raymond Burr television vehicle, and all had
Gardner as the guiding hand.

Details of Gardner at work--since he was paid by the word
for his work for the pulps, he had a gadget on his typewriter
that counted off another tally every time he hit the space bar;
of his struggle to change his style sufficiently to get the
first book published; of his characters (the real reason Della
Street never married Perry Mason, for example); and his philosophy of writing (begin with a mystery and tell a story that
people want to read)--are all to be found in the Fugate book,
published late last year.

It is based primarily on Gardner's papers, transferred *en
masse* to the University of Texas upon his death in 1970. In
this wealth of material lies a fabulous practical how-to-do-it
manual for prospective writers. Gardner's style was function-
al, to say the most. In his mysteries he emphasized plot
above all, which places him slightly out of step in today's
world, but as of 1979 it is reported that he was still averag-
ing 2,400 sales a day, every day of the year.

That Gardner also wrote science fiction will probably come
as a surprise to many, but in *The Human Zero* Gardner's entire
output of fantastic stories is reprinted, all of it vrom *Argosy*
magazine between 1928 and 1932.

As science fiction, from today's perspective, the science
is shaky and the fiction is worse. These seven stories are
filled with mad scientists, strange inventions, catastrophic
calamities, and bizarre theories of evolution. But in those
days between the World Wars this was the nature of the field,
and what Gardner wrote was no worse than any of the rest of
it.

Still, science fiction was obviously not his forte, and he
was probably glad to leave it. Perry Mason was his ticket to
success, not imaginary flights to Venus in backyard anti-gravity
machines.

In essence, what Greenberg and Waugh give us here, in the
first of a series that will reprint much of Gardner's work
from the "woodpulp" pile, are the skeletons of Gardner's past.
Other books may be better. These stories in *The Human Zero*
were probably better left buried.* (*Reviews so marked have
appeared earlier in the Hartford *Courant*.)

Richard Hoyt. *Decoys*. M. Evans, 1980, 203 pp., $8.95.

John Denson is a Seattle private eye. While his first
case is no out-and-out classic, it is refreshingly different,
and Denson's a character I'd love to see again.

Nor would I mind if his competition in this book for an
unknown treasure--unknown to Denson, that is--were to show up
along with him. She is Pamela Yew, also a private investigat-
or, and she knows what the objective is. They make a bet.
She will win the $50,000 piece of artwork adorning Denson's
office. He will win, um, her.

A lot of male/female stuff comes into play. Denson does

not think PI work is a woman's line. She refuses to stay on
the pedestal he offers her. Who wins? You'll have to read
for yourself to find out.
There are also a large number of "decoys" in this book.
It all depends on how deep allegorically you want to dig. And
even so, if you like your detective fiction fast-paced with a
lot of twists, and populated by characters who know what they
are all about, I can't imagine your failing to enjoy this one.
(A minus)

Lesley Egan. *A Choice of Crimes*. Doubleday/Crime Club, 1980,
180 pp.; $8.95.

Filling out the working hours for the detective squad for
the city of Glendale, California, are a series of unsolved
motel robberies, a rapist whose favorite haunt is a darkened
hospital parking lot, various suicides, and all the other many
woes of present-day middle-class suburban America.
Murder is the name of the game, however. According to recent headlines, and incredible 2300 homicides took place in
all of Los Angeles County last year, and some of them are
bound to have happened even in a quiet place like Glendale.
According to this book, it seems to work out to something like
one a day, at the least.
Receiving most of the attention in this shifting mosaic of
cases, switching constantly on and off midstream, are the detective series character team of Vic Varallo and Delia Riordan.
Their work is not described as overly glamorous. It consists
largely of non-stop checking and cross-checking, interviewing,
and endless hours of monotonous legwork.
Resulting from all this intermittent stop-and-go action is
a story without a truly cohesive force to hold it together.
The only discernible focal point is the one case Riordan is
allowed to work on alone, during whatever spare time she can
manage, all the while pondering her choice of life's career.
We have learned what to expect from Lesley Egan. Her police procedurals are always competent and always told from the
Ronald Reagan side of the fence. Although they don't always
win, the cops are unquestionably the heroes here. (C plus)

Joseph Mathewson. *Alicia's Trump*. Avon, 1980, 220 pp., $2.25.

Ellen Nehr recently mentioned that she was looking for
this book on the off chance it had something to do with bridge.
Sorry, Ellen. It doesn't, as you've probably already found
out. Not at all.
I personally happen to feel (as long as you're asking)
that bridge is a hopeless waste of time. It isn't however,
nearly the wast of good intellect as what this book is actually about. Tarot cards.
Ugh. The occult, spiritualism, astronomy, Satanism, or
any combination thereof--I've said it before, and I'm saying
it again: It's all crap. It's pseudoscientific mumbo-jumbo,
the pablum of weak minds incapable of getting through a day
and using an ounce of independent thought at the same time.
It's organized brainrot, on a million dollar scale.
Can you think of a greater contraction in thought processes

than to have the members of a "sort of occult underground" the leading characters in a *detective* novel? You can't begin to imagine how hard it was to force myself to finish this book.

I did, though, and that's only because Mathewson's new sleuth, the elegant Alicia Von Helsing, does not specifically endorse such simple-minded activities herself. The victim, her godson Ronnie, does, or did, and so do most of the suspects in his death.

So, all right. The background *is* one a detective might face. I agree there's no reason why it shouldn't be an appropriate one for a mystery story. But the fact remains, the world of the occult is one that's totally alien to me. I don't understand it, and I just couldn't wait to get out of it.

First in a series, or so it seems. Why a male author (apparently--I won't trap myself completely and say "obviously") would chose to tell a story from the first-person viewpoint of a hip middle-aged married lady from Manhattan is beyond me. The style is fragile and rather brittle, and in Mathewson's hands tends toward the arch and pretentious.

Maybe you'll like it anyway. It isn't bad. I just didn't find it very good. (C)

Marten Cumberland. *The Knife Will Fall.* Doubleday/Crime
   Club, 1943, 263 pp.

In most of the mysteries weitten by Cumberland under his own name, the detective was the formidable Commisaire Saturnin Dax of the French Sureté, so it came as a bit of a surprise to me when I recently discovered that Cumberland was an accomplished English journalist for most of his life and was apparently as British as they come.

(Even less known than Cumberland is today, is the fact that under the pseudonym of Kevin O'Hara he also wrote of the adventures of a London private eye named Chico Brett. None of these books seems ever to have been published in this country.)

In this novel, my own first introduction to the gentleman, the phlegmatic Dax is described as a great bulk of a man; otherwise, our picture of him is reduced and restricted by seeing only his brain at work. If in personality he seems imaginatively dull, his assistant, the English-loving Felix Norman, in strong contrast, does more and reacts more.

The case itself is a peculiarly disjointed one. The connection between a series of victims who seem never to have met or known each other before is the playing card each of them received as an advance warning. One aspect of the case, that of a wife who strangely disappears after being observed reading about the murders in the papers, is even more tenuously tied in.

False clues--red herrings--abound, many of them deliberately set by the gang of killers, led by a mysterious mastermind, or so Dax hypothesizes. The central part of the story sags rather badly. There is no sparkle, no real verve to keep our interest alive. Not until a wholly unexpected killing takes place, taking us by total surprise, are we jolted out of our apathy. The ending is a hodgepodge, but I have to admit that the facts do fit what seemed till then a nearly unexplainable series of events.

A very strange book. Very much out of the ordinary, as if Cumberland had caught the pattern of French thought as well as he seems to have caught the rhythm of the French tongue. (Take this with a grain of salt. I'm no expert on that, either.) (C plus)

Reed Stephens. *The Man Who Killed His Brother*. Ballantine, 1980, 187 pp., $1.95.

Introducing a new private eye, "Brew" Axbrewder, a non-licensed alcoholic who scrapes out a living doing legwork for Ginny Fistoulari, owner and operator of Fistoulari Investigations. The reasons for the title and for his unusual non-employed state of drunken stupor are one and the same--five years ago he accidentally shot and killed his brother, a cop named Rick.

Since he tells his own story, there is a distinct note of whininess that permeates the opening introductions. His brother's thirteen-year-old daughter has mysteriously disappeared, however, and when he discovers it and the action picks up, he seems for a while to feel less sorry for himself.

Together, he and Ginny discover there has been an epidemic of missing young girls, although the police department has quietly kept a lid on the news. Axbrewder's presence on the case promises to change all that, not to everyone's delight.

While in general the characters are shallow and predictable, the events that follow are tough and gritty. When Axbrewder is not engulfed in self-pity, he functions with rough-hewn directness and urgency. He's not a great thinker, though. Maybe it's the effect of being forced to sober up so quickly, but it takes a long while before he puts the clues he finds together.

Will he be a new series character? He could be, but a sequel of any sort at all would have to be built on a new motivation. If not, there is no way possible it could have some of the impact built into this one. It is as if all of Stephens' eggs were in but one basket. (B)

A LATER NOTE: I've since been informed that the author is also Stephen R. Donaldson, a new writer who has done a trilogy of well-regarded fantasy novels reprinted by this same publisher.

Murray Sinclair. *Tough Luck L.A.* Pinnacle, 1980, 243 pp., $2.50.

It's been a while since I read this one. If it weren't for the notes I made while reading it, I don't think I'd remember any of it at all. What makes this so surprising, to me at least, is that I've always been partial to novels about hack Hollywood writers and rundown private eyes, and I was really looking forward to this one.

Anyway. Ben Crandel is the hack writer, making do with cheap porno novels (are there any other kind?) as his movie-writing career seems to be going nowhere fast. Then a friend of his, an ex-prostitute named Vicky, is found murdered, and he's forced to pick up a new sideline, that of amateur detective. Crandel talks snotty to some ultra-sensitive cops, however, and he's immediately tossed into jail for a while.

There is also some business about a tontine. I thought they'd been written off as a plot device long ago. Complications are provided by a complex set of family relationships which I admit I never did figure out, and the whole affair is about as crazy as any pulp novel that's ever been published.

Which, for those of us who dote on such stuff, might have worked out as a huge plus. Dashed with the appropriate amounts of cynicism, there'd have been hopes for this story yet.

The cynicism is contrived and phoney, however, and the pace, which starts out slow and then becomes even slower, never manages to pick up at all.

According to my notes, this is how I felt about it a couple of weeks ago: "Except for one unbelievably imaginative sex scene, the book fairly crackles with boredom."

In retrospect, I don't think it was that bad, but what you could say is that it certainly didn't match my expectations. (D)

Keith Campbell. *Goodbye Gorgeous*. Macdonald, 1952, first published in 1947, 223 pp.

If you're a detective story writer, there are some obvious commercial advantages in having created an established series character to help you sell your books. Not that, for example, either Keith Campbell or his hard-nosed hero, intelligence agent Mike Brett, are exactly what you might call well-known on this side of the Atlantic, but according to Hubin this was the first of at least four of his adventures that have seen print.

I'm wandering from the point. There are some disadvantages to working with a series hero as well. This one begins--considering the chances you have of reading it, I trust I'm not giving too much away--with Brett working incognito as a post-war Canadian ex-Nazi collaborator. Not knowing Brett from Aloysius Dimfuddy, I didn't know. I thought he was. He could have fooled me--and he did. Since this was his first appearance when the book came out, and without a dust jacket to give the whole story away (myself, I never read 'em), I'm sure that I wasn't the only reader who swallowed his story completely.

So here's the point. Campbell/Brett could never pull the same stunt off again, or not nearly as well. As an author, you just don't get a chance like this twice. (Unless you have a hero with a Holmesian penchant for disguises, hmmm?)

To the story. Brett is trying to unravel a plot that may or may not involve a treasure trove hidden by one Joseph Goebbles somewhere in England. There are a couple of women involved (did you doubt it?), and Brett falls for one of them. (And what a surprising lot goes on between the lines!)

The puzzle is an intriguing one for a while, but it fades badly. No surprises. It winds up with a lot of shooting. (C)

Gene Thompson. *Murder Mystery*. Random House, 1980, 275 pp., $9.95.

You have to agree--it's a great title for a detective
story. And for that it's such an obvious one, would you believe that a quick check in Hubin's *Bibliography* would show
that it's the first time it's ever been used?
That, plus the simple elegance of the cover--white on
black with a small insert showing the front of a shiny Rolls
Royce, splattered with blood--would suggest a reading treat
of a highly elite nature about to unfold before us. The
story, however, is a disappointment. It just doesn't measure
up to our expectations. (Well, it didn't mine.)
It tries. While obviously there are very few mean streets
in Malibu, we are nearly persuaded that what lies behind the
doors of some southern California mansions may be insidiously
meaner. Doing the honors as the detective in the case is
society lawyer Dade Cooley, who is persuaded by the daughter
of a client that her mother's fatal accident with her car was
in truth no accident at all.
Well, of course it wasn't. And by actual count, at one
point the list of possible suspects has reached at least
twelve. This is a lot of people to keep close tabs on, and I
fear I lost track of some of them from time to time.
The plot is complex, confusing, and slow-moving. It
hinges at length on a bit of precarious time-tabling that does
manage to get the murderer and the victim together at the same
time, but that is all it does.
As a detective, Cooley is literate and intelligent enough
for the job, but he seems far too fond of himself and his wit
for me to think of him as likable. Thompson may or may not be
making him into a series character--this is apparently his
first murder mystery--but if he is, I'm afraid he's off to a
toe-stubbing start. (C minus)
POSTSCRIPT: There is something else that troubles me about
this book, and maybe I should mention it. One of Thompson's
other characters, not Cooley, is said to have been a poet, and
a few of his lines are quoted to prove it. I have no quarrel
at all with that, of course, but at the end of the book Thompson reveals in a brief acknowledgment that the work in question actually came from the pen of real-life poet Gerard Man-
ley Hopkins. Even if it was reprinted with permission, I
don't know about you, but I'm inclined to think that if this
is meant to be some sort of new literary technique, it's one
we can do without just as quickly.

Hugh Pentecost. *Death After Breakfast*. Dell, 1980, 208 pp.,
    $2.25.

I'm sure that everyone with an interest in paperbacks at
all has seen this new series of Murder Ink/Scene of the Crime
mysteries from Dell. Chosen by the respective proprietresses
of two of the country's first specialized mystery bookshops,
so far the series has emphasized detective novels of a recent
vintage over Golden Age reprints. Even so, there have been a
few of them included among the ones I received so far, notably
Anthony Berkeley's *The Poisoned Chocolates Case* and A.A.
Milne's *The Red House Mystery*.
And, to back up just a little bit, the word "detective"
should have been emphasized in the sentence just above. This
book by Hugh Pentecost comes as close as any of them have been

in being straight "action fiction."

Of those others I'm familiar with, those which are reprints of recent hardcover mysteries, there seems to have been a noticeable attempt on the part of their authors to add a sizeble amount of characterization to their work--and in some cases, like *The Brandenburg Hotel*, by Pauline Glen Winslow, and *McGarr and the Sienese Conspiracy*, by Bartholomew Gill, this seems to have been done at the expense of the plot, unfortunately. (That both of these books were chosen by Carol Brener at Murder Ink does not seem wholly relevant, or at least not yet.)

This one is a Scene of the Crime selection, and I missed it when it came out in hardcover. What else can I say? Everyone should read a Pierre Chambrun novel sometime, but other than that there seems to be no reason at all why anyone would want to read more than one.

Even when he turns up missing, as he does in the first half of this one, the Hotel Beaumont (of which he is the manager) might go on running as smoothly as ever for a while, but that's only another measure of how completely his personality dominates the scene.

In his absence, the nymphomaniac chairwoman of the Cancer Fund Ball is found brutally murdered in her room, and a bomb threat is taken very seriously.

Pentecost is, if nothing else, always smooth and easy to read. The greatest handicap he faces in continuing the Chambrun series, of which there are a great number already, is the enormous effort and amount of maneuvering required to get all the principals in his coolly-calculated melodramas together under one roof, even one as large as the Beaumont's. (C)

Thomas J. Green. *The Flowered Box*. Beaufort Books, 1980, 187 pp., $9.95.

The publication of a hardcover book being the expensive proposition it must be today, you don't really expect to find one any more that doesn't even come up to, say, third-rank paperback standards.

Still, by any interpretation you may make of the word probability, even the unlikeliest of events has to happen once in a while, and it takes only one example to prove the point. And, as it so happens, you needn't look any further. I have one, right here.

In it the Boston police are so busy chasing a cop killer that the mysterious death of a derelict wino doesn't interest them at all. They slough off the case to two unorthodox amateur private eyes named Caro Borsa dna Aaron Gates. Borsa is Italian, as you might have guessed, and Gates is black,

The victim turns out to have been a Viet Nam defector who has sneaked back into the United States for some unknown reason. The cops know this, but somehow it's still not enough to keep them interested in the case. The only clue Borsa and Gates have to work with is a small empty box the dead man had just sent his sister in Philadelphia while he was still in his refuge in Denmark.

So what's wrong with the book, you ask? Well, first of all, we don't really need another pair of unorthodox detectives, do we? We get our fill of that on television, or at

least I do. The two heroes here do a lot of running around
Boston, and Copenhagen, and we see a lot of nice scenery, but
other than that the purpose or usefulness of all this activity
is not always easy to say.

And the dialogue--ah, yes, the dialogue--what it reminded
me most of was none other than Frank and Joe Hardy, working on
their latest mystery in good old Bayport. (Don't get me wrong.
I'm not making light of the cases they solved at all. I simply devoured them myself when I was a kid, and I still have a
lot of fond memories wrapped up in them, but--and tell me the
truth--if you're over fifteen, when was the last time you actually read one?)

People in this story seem to have a pronounced aversion to
simply saying their words. They exclaim, they interrupt, they
urge, they shrug, they query, they gush, they bellow, they
smile, they rebut, and more. (And all within the space of
about six pages, he added.) (D minus)

Barbara D'Amato. *The Hands of Healing Murder*. Charter, 1980,
248 pp., $2.50.

For a first novel, and a paperback original at that, this
book turns out to have a surprising number of things going for
it. It also succeeds in going against the current flow of
action/suspense/horror fiction in being a decently presented
work of *detective* fiction. (Note the emphasis.)

The detective is Dr. Gerritt DeGraaf, a pathologist who
happens to be there at the scene of the first murder. He also
happens to be a close friend of Inspector Craddock, and this
allows him to channel his bubbling enthusiasm for life and the
challenge of the impossible into solving the case as well.

The victim dies in a room where eight other people are
playing duplicate bridge, although not in full view of any of
them. The fingerprints on the murder weapon belong to none of
them, however, and as it happens, no one else could have en-
tered the room. In short, the impossible has happened.

Some interesting discussion of the technology of fingerprints eventually takes place. A question of morality also
comes up--that which underlies the constant problem faced by
doctors whenever they must decide who it is who lives and who
will die in the confrontation of both limited time and limited
resources.

The story is obviously intelligently written, if not always imaginatively. It is Craddock who tells the story, and
sometimes this is awkward, as there are parts of it which he
can tell only as hearsay. It is also not quite clear when
De-Graaf has the solution, and the hint of late-blooming romance (storywise) seems oddly out of place.

Overall, however, a cozy, comfortable sort of detective
story, which, coincidentally enough, I was exactly in the mood
for when I read it. It's certainly an above average debut,
and one definitely not to be missed if Agatha Christie, for
example, is your idea of a perfect "10." (B plus)

Demouzon. *Mouche*. Peebles Press/The Midnight Library, 1979,
244 pp., $8.95; first published in French in 1976.

It doesn't happen very often, but once in a while in the world of detective fiction there do turn up private eyes we soon learn we'll see only once. They become so involved personally in their one case on record that we know without a doubt that we'll never see them again.

Such a one is Robert Flecheux, of the Bureau Clairival. He is hired by an old woman to find her granddaughter, but she dies before he can even start on the case. After thinking it over, he decides that circumstances warrant his staying on the trail, if only for a while.

The scent leads him to Paris, and the pornographic movie industry there, and to a house where it is said that even more sensational thrills are available. Death also follows Flecheux's trail, and he begins to realize that his hunch about Mme. Mouchardou's untimely demise was a good one.

Irony is described as part of Flecheux's everyday nature, as if we could not have been expected to discover it on our own. Demouzon does not seem to realize how much more effective a subtler disguise would have been.

Nor is the final solution as shocking as Demouzon says it is, which of course again is precisely the flaw he does not see. It fails because he *says* it is shocking, and because he cannot make the reader feel it as well.

Flecheux ends up looking like an amateur in a game which he has chosen as his life's work. He commits too many fatal errors, and he is far too guilty of endless introspection. Blame it on too much involvement, if you will (and read the first paragraph again).

Let me repeat myself, however. We are simply told that this is so, and we are never really allowed to feel it for ourselves. (C)

Sheila Radley. *The Chief Inspector's Daughter*. Scribner's, 1980, 208 pp., $8.95.

The inspector's name is Quantrill, and you may have met him before in *Death in the Morning*. That one I haven't read myself, but I'm going to. This one's a good one.

To tell you the truth, though, I wasn't so sure it was going to be when I started. The first couple of chapters are not all that promising. Stories involving British policemen and their dreary home lives I find more-or-less depressing. A little bit of it, at least, usually goes a long way.

Apparently, vital communications between Quantrill and his wife have been gradually breaking down over the years, and to compound the problem their younger daughter has just arrived home from London after a break-up with her lover. Nothing like a good case of murder to bring a family together, hmmm?

But that's just what it does. Daughter Alison takes a job as an assistant to Jasmine Woods, a well-known writer of romantic fiction. When Alison finds her employer brutally murdered one morning, she goes into shock, and then she disappears before revealing the important clue she knows.

Some of the best clues in this story are provided by the simple expedient of omission, however, and you as reader are going to have to stay on your toes to stay ahead of the game. The plotting is rather cleverly done, but Sheila Radley plays fair, and you really do have a good chance of beating Quantrill to the killer.

I liked the ending. While it has nothing to do with the mystery, per se, I think by story's end the characters have indeed become reasonable enough facsimilies of human beings for it to be considered one of the best cliffhanger finales in quite some time. (B plus)

E.X. Ferrars. *Frog in the Throat.* Doubleday/Crime Club, 1980, 185 pp., $8.95.

Although E.X. Ferrars has been writing mysteries for over forty years, she's no where as well-known as she should be. One big reason I can see for that is that since her first five books, not until very recently has she used a series character of any kind. (And of Toby Dyke, who has not been heard from since 1942, I know nothing at all.)

Where would Christie have been without Poirot or Miss Marple? Ingenious mystery plots may be totally fine in the abstract, but unfortunately they just don't grab the reader's attention in the bookstore.

There is a bare chance--but don't count on it--that Virginia Freer's errant ex-husband Felix, who has appeared at least one time before†, may return again and "solve" another case. He slips in and out of her life with such casualness that it is not a foregone conclusion that he will. Nor is his idea of finding a killer a very useful one for the police.

Dead is a writer of historical novels, on the night of her engagement party to poet Basil Deering, who is the murderer's next target. Or are there two murderers? A bigamous marriage some years in the past seems to be the crux of the matter, as well as some other more recent romantic entanglements, and a bit of injudicious blackmail.

The ending is vaguely unsatisfying. Perhaps just a bit of a letdown. I think it's because it's clear that the police this time are perfectly capable of solving the murders by themselves, without the odd-couple assistance of Mr. and Mrs. Freer.

On the other hand, while the fuss they generate may not have been wholly necessary, it is nonetheless a fascinating and wholly absorbing sort of fuss. (And why else do we read mysteries?) (B)

†I am a little confused on this point. The dust jacket says that Virginia Freer appeared in *In at the Kill,* which I have not read, but a quick glimpse-through does not show me that she has any great part. I can confirm the fact, however, that both Freers do appear in *Last Will and Testament.*

Paul Ruse. *The Alumni Murders.* Tower, 1980, 254 pp., $1.95.

This is a page-turner. While obviously as exploitative as horror movies such as "Prom Night," which just played here on network television, here is a book that, in its own way, you may find equally difficult to let loose of.

And the story is very nearly the same. To revenge a hurt inflicted years in the past, someone is hunting down and killing those judged responsible. This time the story takes place

at a high school reunion party, somewhere by a small lake in
Kansas.
The killer is unknown, but once the deaths begin, easily
spotted. What I found most remarkable was that the characters,
while sometimes crudely and pulpishly drawn, were actually
strong enough to command my attention all the long while before the first killing takes place, fully seventy percent of
the way into the book. (C plus)

Richard Forrest. *The Death at Yew Corner*. Holt, Rinehart &
    Winston, 1980, 172 pp., $10.95.

Connecticut's own amateur sleuthing team of Bea and Lyon
Wentworth are back at it again. This is the fifth case they've
tackled in tandem, which doesn't yet put them into the super-
star category of a Mr. and Mrs. North, but it is enough to
start attracting them some attention.
In this one Bea, who has just lost her bid for a state con-
gressional seat, finds a place to vent her energies when an
old friend dies in a mysterious nursing home accident. Join-
ing her in her investigation is her husband, Lyon, author of
all those marvelous children's stories about the Wobblies.
Murphysville, which may or may not be Middletown in disguise, is also the scene of an ugly ongoing confrontation between the management of the convalescent home and its angry,
militant employees. There is a connection, as Bea sood discovers.
A surprising number of other bizarre deaths follow, cul-
minating in the fascinating puzzle of a murder committed in
a locked bathroom. Just as you begin to think that the book
has gone off the deep end completely, however, author Richard
Forrest suddenly snaps everything into place, and what's more
he makes it look easy.
Bea Wentworth, as the star of the show, may remind you a
bit of TV's ultra-liberal Maude, from the series of the same
name. Bea, however, is not nearly as prone to loud histrion-
ics to make her point. In spite of various and sundry tempta-
tions, she manages to stay her level-headed best in this out-
ing, and she helps pull it off rather nicely. (B)*

Mary Challis. *Crimes Past*. Raven House, 1980, 188 pp., $1.75.

Just by coincidence, if you believe in such things, I got
a letter from Al Hubin yesterday, and he admits he doesn't
know who "Mary Challis" is either. (But if there's anyone
else who'd be more sure of ferreting out the truth, I don't
know who it might be.)
According to the back cover, Mary Challis is the pseudonym
of a writer with more than thirty mysteries to her credit.
She also lives in London, Ontario, if that helps. If this
book is an example of her work, however, I think I'll pass on
the thirty others, thank you.
There are twelve chapters in this book, and I warn you,
Chapter 11 is a complete waste of time. I've heard of padding
before, but this is ridiculous. The culprit is known on page
162. One suspects, even eagerly awaits the surprise twist...
but... there is none. There is absolutely nothing of impor-

tance that happens in the next twenty pages.

It hadn't been a particularly gripping story even up to then. It seems that lawyer Jeremy Locke's brother has returned to England after fourteen years of self-imposed exile. He fled the country when he did to avoid imprisonment on embezzlement charges. No one has ever found the money, and now one of Derek Locke's old comrades is found murdered.

Jeremy, who is thirty years old and eight years a lawyer, acts like a gawky, teen-aged kid. With the police; with his guardian and senior partner; with his older brother, whe he finally shows up; and with his new girl friend, Lisa Marlowe, who is also the secretary of a mystery writer named Stephen Jackson.

Mr. Jackson is mentioned once or twice more, but nothing ever comes of it. What a shame. His presence might have done something (anything!) to waken up this sleepy, placid little novel. (D)

Robert B. Parker. *Early Autumn*. Delacorte/Seymour Lawrence, 1981, 212 pp., $10.95.
●

In the world of detective fiction, Spenser has to be the best private eye going. He's already won author Robert Parker one Edgar, for *Promised Land*, and another is long since due.

Spenser works the Boston area. His interest is always in justice, no matter how rough-shod the methods. The result is admittedly not always a detective story, as defined by common usage, nor even a mystery story per se. To the dismay and displeasure of purists, Parker's interest lies in his characters. Even whatever crimes are involved can be peripheral to the story.

Case in point. Spenser is hired by a boy's mother to retrieve him from his father. They are divorced. The kid is a pawn. Neither parent wants him; neither wants the other to have him.

To effect the salvation of Paul Giacomin, who is fifteen and shrugs a lot, Spenser decides to keep him himself. To make him autonomous--he obviously cannot count on his parents to make anything of him--Spenser teaches him what he knows. Boxing, camping, building.

To maintain the summer's progress, he needs more. A little blackmail helps. It also helps that the boy's parents have secrets. It isn't all lovey-dovey kissy-poo stuff. To Spenser, the kid's life is at stake, and there's no need for kid gloves.

Spenser knows who he is, what his rules for himself are, and that he'll always have to break them because rules don't always work. What most people follow, to his mind, are the rules of others, as they try in vain to fit well-defined categories.

Not only is Robert Parker an exceedingly fine writer, who can convince you that such an approach to child-raising is not only possible, but also probably necessary, but his approach to fiction follows the same philosophy. It's early, but so far, this is the best book I've read this year. (A plus)*

Verdicts
(More Reviews)

Joe L. Hensley. *Outcasts*. Doubleday, 1981, 180 pp., $9.95.

From the evidence of best-seller lists and paperback racks it would seem that there are only two subjects in today's crime-suspense novels: neo-Nazis plotting Wolrl War III and terrorists with nukes holding Metropolis for ransom. But traditional mystery fiction still (praise be) exists, although out of choice or necessity many of its practitioners write whodunits as a second career while holding down regular jobs elsewhere.

One of the best mystery moonlighters is Indiana trial judge Joe L. Hensley, whose ninth novel like several before it features fighting criminal lawyer Don Robak. In *Outcasts,* Robak comes into a small mid-western city to defend his cousin, a former policeman who had been framed and kicked off the force by corrupt local pols, and who has now been charged with and again claims he's being framed for the brutal murder of his girlfriend. The city's economy depends on a luxury resort hotel which covertly offers every vice to its affluent patrons, and like crusading lawyers in earlier Hensley novels, Robak has to cope with harassment from police, politicians, and suspects with secrets as he tries to clear his client prior to trial.

Tearing the lid off the crooked city is a time-honored theme in American crime fiction, but Hensley downplays the expected elements of action, suspense, and menace and keeps his novel quiet, low-key, unhurried, unhysterical, stressing character interplay among typical mid-western folk rather than Chandler's "streets dark with something more than night." But he never forgets that it's a mystery novel he's writing, and events build subtly toward the exposure of a truly surprising Least Likely Suspect at the climax. Readers not in the mood for High Anxiety Superthriller #6723-G will enjoy spending an evening in Hensley's unfrenetic mid-American world. (Mike Nevins)

George V. Higgins. *The Rat on Fire*. Knopf, 1981, 183 pp., $10.95.

The crime novels of George V. Higgins seem governed by rules as unalterable as the movement of the tides. The set-

ting is Boston and suburbs, the milieu is that of small-time
crooks and their hangers-on, the slender plot is a hook on
which hangs Higgins' portrait of the business and personal
lives of various two-legged toads, the dialogue of each and
every character is rich in circumlocutions and obscenities and
loutish urban wit so that it's sometimes a chore for us to
tell them apart. *The Rat on Fire* lives up to expectations ad-
mirably. In Higgins' usual nonlinear fashion we follow the
progress of a conspiracy between a corrupt fire marshal, a
besieged slumlord and a professional arsonist to torch a put-
refying apartment building in Boston's black ghetto--and the
simultaneous efforts of three cops who are shadowing the con-
spirators to get enough evidence to arrest them before the
blaze is actually set. It's a knowing look at the mechanics
and economics of arson, the roots of urban blight, the pressure of inflation on ethics, and the bizarre, irrational, im-
possibly screwed-up nature of life in general, told almost entirely in Higgins' unique brand of pungent dialogue. Economic
compulsion tries to make rats of us all, he seems to say, but
we are still responsible if we give in. Higgins rarely leaves
readers feeling good but never fails to make us think--and
squirm. (Mike Nevins)

Richard Hugo. *Death and the Good Life*. St. Martin's Press,
1981, 215 pp., $10.95.

Twenty-odd years ago Ross Macdonald permanently trans-
formed the landscape of private-eye fiction by dispensing with
dark alleys and gangsters and macho mannerisms and making his
protagonist Lew Archer a contemplative, compassionate man in-
vestigating crimes of the present with deep psychological
roots in the past. So attractive were the later Archer novels
that virtually every private-eye writer since then has felt
compelled to turn out the same kind of book, each with his own
personal variation on the protagonist: a black or Jewish or
homosexual or cowardly Archer. The eminent poet Richard Hugo
has now joined the army of change-ringers on Macdonald themes
with his first crime novel, in which the Archer figure is not a
private eye at all but a cop--the softest-hearted, gentlest
cop in the literature.
After seventeen years on the Seattle force, Al Barnes
takes early retirement and moves to western Montana where he
becomes a small-town deputy under a fat, cigar-chomping Indian
sheriff. The quiet peach of the northwest is shattered by a
series of brutal axe murders apparently committed by a six-
and-a-half-foot-tall woman maniac, but Mush Heart Barnes has
caught the lady before page 50, and then the real story begins.
For it soon becomes clear that one of the axe murders in the
series was not the woman's but the work of an imitator hoping
to bury his own crime in the tangle of hers. And the hunt for
the imitator takes Barnes to the wealthy suburbs of Portland,
Oregon, where, indistinguishable from an Archeresque private
eye and showing no awareness of proper police procedure, he
exposes the secret vices of the rich and reopens a twenty-
year-old murder case which will shatter the lives of everyone
it touches.
Hugo writes simply and unpretentiously, with a bare min-
imum of linguistic color, and plots like the architect of the

labyrinth. The northwestern scenes are vividly evoked and the incidental character sketches softly quirky, like the tough Portland homicide captain and the wily criminal defense lawyer who on the side are both published poets. If only one could believe in Hugo's detective! With his overwhelming gentleness, his optimism about human nature, his feelings of guilt for the world's woes, his sudden subliminal intuitions, his habit of sharing his innermost thoughts with murder suspects, his bizarre notion of a Miranda warning ("I'm placing you under arrest. You know your rights because you're rich"), Al Barnes simply fails to come across as any sort of credible cop. But if Hugo has failed to transform police fiction along Ross Macdonald lines he has at least given us a fascinating potpourri of a first mystery novel, not totally satisfying but well worth a read nonetheless. (Mike Nevins)

Simon Brett. *The Dead Side of the Mike*. Scribner's, 1980, 176 pp., $8.95.

The amateur sleuth of English mysteries is still almost always a man, but he's not the man he used to be. During the golden age of British detective fiction, in the recess between World Wars, he tended to be a brilliant intellectual, full of literary quotations and upper-class snobbishness, his lifestyle comfortable to elegant thanks to independent income, his friends sprinkled throughout the established institutions he so clearly revered, his emotions (such as they were) always under control. That world has long since passed away, and the amateur detective of contemporary Britain is much more likely to be less of an intellectual giant, less financially secure, living in drab quarters, lusting for small pleasures, his emotional life all askew, but still a man of fundamental decency with a thirst to know the truth. One of the best of this vanishing species is is Charles Paris, the fiftyish minor actor and accidental sleuth whose adventures are chronicled by Simon Brett.

Brett worked in the English entertainment industries for several years and his five previous novels about Paris have been set in the theater and other media. The setting for his sixth book is BBC Radio, in one of whose editing booths a beautiful young studio manager has apparently committed suicide by slashing her wrists. Paris's rather leisurely investigation gives us a richly satiric yet informative portrait of life at the Beeb and the production of various kinds of programs, and the trim but neatly twisty plot climaxes with a night chase through the hallowed corridors of Broadcasting House.

The British radio jargon takes a bit of getting used to, but Brett explains it all quite clearly except for failing to tell U.S. readers that the producer of an English program is in American parlance the director. When Brett introduces American suspects and incidents into the plot, the dialogue alternates between straight British idiom and that bizarre dialect so dear to English writers who can't get on paper the way we in the States talk. But otherwise this is a fine example of the clever, contemporary mustery from across the Atlantic, solved by one of the most interesting and well-drawn detective characters of recent years. (Mike Nevins)

Jonathan Valin. *Final Notice*. Dodd Mead, 1980, 246 pp.,
$8.95.

The private detective as a protagonist in crime fiction is
almost sixty years old. As a force in the popular literature
he has survived the Depression, World War II, the Cold War,
and the turmoil of the Sixties and Seventies, and he is still
in there punching today. He never existed in real life any
more than did the cowboy heroes of countless Western films,
but as a mythical archetype, a symbol of gritty integrity in a
dirty urban world, he is just as crucial to America's under-
standing of itself.
     Jonathan Valin, until last year a teacher of creative writ-
ing at Washington University, has launched the first new private eye series of the Eighties with the adventures of Cincinnati based Harry Stoner, who debuted earlier this year in the
critically acclaimed *The Lime Pit*. Harry is not the standard
wisemouth macho derived from Bogart but a quietly sensitive
professional and something of a moralist in the tradition of
Ross Macdonald's Lew Archer. His cases, however, are anything
but quiet and tend to involve him in extremes of graphic violence. *Final Notice*, in which Harry hunts the connection between some mutilated art books in a suburban public library
and the mutilated body of a young woman art student in a city
park, demonstrates as did *The Lime Pit* that Valin has few
peers at describing freshly butchered human beings. The story
starts slowly but builds well, providing Harry with a liberat-
ed young woman as partner in detection and romance during the
search through various levels of Cincinnati society for the
Ripper who is preparing to slash again. The book's best scene
is the brutal *mano a mano* between Harry and a muscle-bound
psychotic in a muddy barnyard, but the most unusual aspect of
this series is the way the protagonist's character contrasts
with the environment of slaughter that surrounds him. He
breaks little new ground, but Jonathan Valin is well on the
way to becoming one of the more reliable private eye writers
of the new decade. It's good to have him with us. (Mike
Nevins)

Guy M. Townsend, John J. McAleer, Judson C. Sapp, and Arriean
     Schemer. *Rex Stout: An Annotated Primary and Secondary
     Bibliography*. Garland, 1980, 199 pp., $30.

The first thing I noted (after recovering from the blind
staggers induced by the price) was that the paper was good for
250 years--with craftsmanship to match! (No mean compliment,
considering the books produced today.)
     After an excellent (but unattributed) introduction that
covers Stout's life and a sample of commentary on the Wolfe
stories, the book gets down to business. It is logically and
systematically arranged in sixteen sections that deal various-
ly with Stout's writings (novels, short stories, poetry,
jacket blurbs, etc.), movies and pastiches, etc., and inter-
views and criticisms. Each section is arranged chronological-
ly and most entries (except omnibuses, etc.) have short synop-
ses of content. As far as possible, all editions (both hard
and paper) of each work are listed--complete with book number
for paperbacks. Reviews follow each entry. Those that have

been read are rated + (positive, - (negative), or +/- (mixed)--
an entertaining detail. The book is pulled together with a
comprehensive index to make this a truly useful reference.
Two separate appendices are provided for Wolfe novels and
short stories.

Mandatory for those possessed of Stout/Wolfe mania. Op-
tional for the Wolfe fan. Probably too expensive for the oc-
casional reader of Stout. (Linda Toole)

David Skene Melvin and Ann Skene Melvin. *Crime, Detective,
Espionage, Mystery, and Thriller Fiction & Film: A Compre-
hensive Bibliography of Critical Writing through 1979.*
Greenwood Press, 367 pp., $29.95.

Now that the field of mystery fiction has suddenly achieved
status after more than one hundred years of being considered
as second-class literature, we are blessed with an exciting
plethora of commentary and reference material. Half the fun
of reading whodunits, howdunits, and whydunits is reading
about them and their authors. But, like the mysteries themselves, much of this supplementary material has been hidden
from view and hard to ferret out even though the amount of new
and significantly important material published is now rapidly
increasing. This very well done bibliography will identify
such material and make it accessible to mystery fans as well
as to students and scholars of the genre and will bring to
your attention much that has been published in obscure publi-
cations. Included are articles and books on not only the detective story, but also police procedural and crime psychology
stories, spy novels, thriller and related adventure tales, and
films. It is wide-ranging, covering more than 1600 items from
twenty-five countries, in eighteen languages. Entries are
listed by author in alphabetical order giving full bibliographical description (including page numbers if published in
a periodical), followed by an alphabetical title index, a subject index, and an index identifying those published in other
than the English language. The subject index is far-reaching,
including author and title critiques as well as subjects and
topics. This volume is attractively printed and bound, and
should become a well-used and standard reference work. It will
open many new vistas to the mystery fan and is highly recom-
mended. Thank you, David Skene Melvin and Ann Skene Melvin
for making this available! (Michael L. Cook)

Donald Zochert. *Murder in the Hellfire Club.* Penguin, 1980,
240 pp., $2.95.

To the writing of stories of detection set in Victoria's
time, there seems to be no end. Here, however, is one set in
Georgian times--George II, that is. A group of rakes who have
organized some of their debaucheries under the name of the
Hellfire Club seem to be threatened with systematic extinction.
Despite the date's being 1757, it appears that one of the de-
bauchees has been electrocuted. The only man in the world who
could possibly solve this crime is that quintessential American, Benjamin Franklin. Displaying in the process a vastly
detailed knowledge of the period, Mr. Zochert sends gentle Ben

kiting around London in pursuit of the murderer. There are
several more corpses and the chase winds through the twisting
streets of London, in and around orgies, past many a buxom
wench, and up the Thames to a spread-eagled Iron Maiden before
justice is meted out by the usual higher authority.

To my mind, Mr. Zochert is more successful at recreating
the minutiæ , the world of chambermaids and chamberpots, than
at breathing life into Ben Franklin and the assorted rakehells.
The plot is labyrinthine and the action far from lightning
fast. Further, one finds it difficult to be too concerned
with the fate of such unpleasant men. One wonders what Franklin himself, whose own prose was so unadorned, would have made
of the elevated style in which much of this book is written.
In the last judgment, *Murder in the Hellfire Club* is an interesting misfire. (Carl Larsen)

Dorothy B. Hughes. *The Expendable Man.* New York: Random
House, 1963.

Dr. Hugh Densmore, an intern who is driving alone through
the desolate wastes between Los Angeles and Phoenix on his way
to his niece's wedding, is inexplicably tense about being
harassed by a car full of teen-agers. Later, despite what
seems exaggerated concern, he picks up a lone hitchhiker, a
girl of about fifteen who is crude and none too clean. When
he drops her off, he is excessively relieved, but later she
forces herself on him again, taking advantage of his pity and
vulnerability. He is, however, adamant in his refusal to per-
form the abortion she finally demands.

Hugh's forebodings are justified when the girl's body is
found and an anonymous tip to the police connects him to her.
Finally we learn the reason for his earlier fears, and the joy
of his niece's wedding festivities is contrasted with his
deepening sense of impending disaster. Other characters are a
lovely young woman, another wedding guest to whom he is immediately attracted, a bigoted and brutal policeman, a fair
and objective county marshal, and a brilliant and ambitious
lawyer.

Suspense builds inescapably as Hugh is harassed by an
anonymous enemy and badgered by the police, while he tries to
protect his family from any knowledge of his plight. The
solution to the mystery of the girl's death comes finally as a
result of discoveries made separately by Hugh's lawyer and by
the police, but Hugh's own investigations provide the key.

The novel is tautly plotted, and characterization, especially of the innocent but vulnerable man with his reputation
and future career in danger, is effectively handled. Recom-
mended. (Mary Jean DeMarr)

Sheila Radley. *Death in the Morning.* Dell, 1980, 256 pp.

Recently promoted to Detective Chief Inspector at Breckham
Market Division Headquarters, Douglas Quantrill faces several
problems at the opening of Sheila Radley's *Death in the Morning*. As always, the department's books are overloaded with a
raft of unsolved crimes, and one especially, the disappearance
of fifteen-year-old Joy Dawson, preys on his mind. Also, he

is just beginning the process of breaking in a new man, Detective Sergean Martin Tait.

When Mary Gedge is found drowned, Quantrill and Tait work
together on the case, despite the tensions between them. Not
only is young Tait a city man, now working in a countryside to
which he is ill-suited, but also he is the product of university and police college training. Quantrill, on the other
hand, is a middle-aged copper who left school at fourteen and
is uneasy and self-conscious about his lack of formal educa-
tion. Despite the irritations which arise between the two
policemen, their pairing is bad luck for the killer, for they
make a good team.

In fact, their separate insights are exactly what are
needed to solve the murder, for Mary Gedge's death is a peculiar blend of violence and peaceful, pastoral romanticism.
Gathering flowers along the edge of the extremely shallow
local river, Mary has apparently encountered someone known and
supposedly friendly who has held the youngster's head firmly
under water until she drowns. The body is found floating
Ophelia-like amid the broken blossoms of Mary's May Day bouquet.
Because Mary has no known enemies, indeed she's been a kind of
brilliant, innocent, village golden girl, the investigators
are forced into serious and productive personality studies of
all the unlikely suspects--her brother, local swains, two of
her male teachers.

One of the best sources of background information about
Mary is Jean Bloomfield, her former headmistress and friend.
Bloomfield, a widow, and the DCI have encountered one another
in the past, during a period when Douglas Quantrill and his
wife were separated, their marriage damaged by the pressures
of his job and the erosion of time. Ever since, Quantrill has
cherished a romantic love for Bloomfield, and their relationship forms an important subplot. Further, the Quantrill marriage, now stabilized but still unfulfilling, is contrasted
with the dreary marital affairs of Mary's brother, Derek, who
has been trapped into wedlock by his sluttish, pregnant sweet-
heart. Both couples are badly matched, and part of the tension of the plot stems from the male partners' efforts to com-
promise or to set themselves free.

An important theme is loneliness: Derek Gedge, Jean Bloomfield and Douglas all struggle with that problem, and all are
introspective enough to identify it and to analyze their own
feelings. Quantrill, as a private citizen, is, of course,
especially interested in Jean Bloomfield's situation, for he
is still deeply in love with her.

> It occurred to Quantrill, for the first time, that a woman in
> a position of authority and responsibility, who lives alone in a
> small community where social life is geared to families or couples,
> must almost inevitably feel lonely.
>
> But loneliness is not exclusive to women. And you can be just
> as lonely, he knew, inside marriage as out of it. Lonelier, some-
> times.

Radley uses both Quantrill's and Tait's points of view
with great success. The clues are presented fairly and un-
obtrusively, and the several passages depicting violent deaths
in the various characters' past lives echo the motif of violence beneath the surface of daily village life, making that

old pattern fresh yet again. Inevitably, the mystery of Mary Gedge's death *is* solved, but, realistically, the disappearance of Joy Dawson remains an open case--and serves as a frame story. For all these reasons, *Death in the Morning* is a satisfying mystery; Sheila Radley has done a good job. (Jane S. Bakerman)

Anthony Gilbert. *The Spinster's Secret*. Collins, 1956.

Anthony Gilbert [Lucy Beatrice Malleson] is always good for a pleasant, relaxing yarn, and *The Spinster's Secret* (first published in 1946) is no exception; it's worth going back to. Gilbert is accomplished at building tension, sustaining suspense, and developing swift, fascinating action. All those qualities are deftly handled, but, also as usual, Gilbert adds her extra fillip: characters who are charming and appealing-- and just short of zany or cute. It's a hard balance to achieve, but Gilbert manages it.

Here, as in most of her novels, Gilbert creates a hero and a protagonist. The hero is her continuing character, lawyer Arthur Crook; the protagonist is the spinster of the title, Miss Martin. Miss Martin becomes friendly with little Pamela, the orphaned ward of a wealthy invalid, and Pamela's governess, young, pretty Terry Lawrence. The friendship is a real comfort to the lonely old lady until Pamela suddenly disappears. This loss is quickly followed by another blow; Miss Martin is remanded to a particularly unsavory "home" for aged women. Then, Miss Martin spots Pamela, now also institutionalized, subdued, and renamed "Mary," and the old woman's efforts to solve the mystery of Pamela's transformation throw her and Terry into deadly danger. Naturally, Crook appears on the scene to straighten things out.

What keeps Miss Martin, Terry, and Pamela from sugary sweetness are their determination and spunk. Both women love the child and are firmly resolved to help her. Pamela has no one else; both her champions know that, and they respond to the little girl's need. But sentiment is not the only factor in their cause; they are also committed to doing the right, the honorable, thing--and they are tough and practical in their actions.

They do need, however, the loud, flamboyant Arthur Crook, lawyer for criminals as well as for distressed ladies of all ages. Crusty and eccentric on the outside, Crook is soft and eccentric on the inside. His tactics are as brazen and extreme as they are effective--and he's very great fun.

Gilbert is not afraid of creating female villains, and nothing is given away by saying that she does so here, carrying her device of dual identities to a surprising but logical conclusion. For Gilbert's established fans, these meanies will be readily recognizable but still fresh. For new readers, they'll be a good introduction. *The Spinster's Secret*, like almost any Crook adventure, is worth a raid on your local secondhand bookshop. (Jane S. Bakerman)

Margaret Yorke. *The Point of Murder*. Arrow, 1980.

Margaret Yorke's *The Point of Murder* is an inverted mystery, the suspense arising from the contest between protagonist and antagonist. The tone is rather cold, in keeping with the personality of the protagonist, Kate Wilson, and with the calculating if disorganized mind of the killer. Despite Yorke's tendency to tell readers key insights, ideas, and information instead of showing them through fully dramatized scenes, the book succeeds. The pace is, by and large, well maintained; the scenes Yorke chooses to depict carry the story adequately, and the cool tone wards off unappealing sentimentality.

On the surface, Kate Wilson is meek, plain and uninteresting, the efficient, unimaginative "Girl Friday" to a panel of physicians and the slave of her mother, who has "chosen never to recover from the shock of Kate's birth when Mrs. Wilson was forty-four years old and had long since abandoned hope of a replacement for the son who had died in infancy fifteen years before." Mrs. Wilson is a stereotypical domineering mother, as unsavory as they come, and, at first, Kate appears to be typical of all the repressed daughters in fiction.

But beneath the surface there is another Kate. As a means of intermittent, temporary escape from her mother, Kate has developed a false identity. For secret weekends away from home (her mother thinks she's visiting a school friend), Kate becomes the poised Mrs. Havant, complete with fancy hairdo, different wardrobe--and a lover.

It is on one of those weekends that Kate sees the murderer and his victim together. When news of the murder appears in the press, Kate struggles with her conscience--helping the police will mean blowing Mrs. Havant's cover. While Kate tries to bring herself to the point of confession, the killer is once again trying to bring himself to the point of murder; he remembers Kate and sets out to track her down. The reader follows the thoughts of both characters as the pressure on each mounts and the personalities of both are quite fully revealed.

We learn quite a bit about Kate--she does have a conscience, and, usually, she is capable of fast, direct action, but she very much wants to preserve those weekends of comfort and passion and she needs the refuge of Mrs. Havant's personality and habits because she is unwilling to face her mother down and achieve real freedom. She needs secrecy because she's afraid she'll be dropped from her mother's will. The inheritance will be modest, but Kate feels she's earned it in servitude to her mother--and revelation will not only blow her cover but also earn her mother's fury. As Kate weighs her obligations against the consequences, a very interesting level of her personality is revealed: to a certain degree, she shares her mother's calculating nature. This trait helps account, oddly enough, for her affair as well as for the book's climax.

Parallel to Kate's character revelation is that of the murderer, Gary Browne. An encyclopedia salesman, Gary has been as eagerly self-indulgent as Kate has been reluctantly self-denying, and readers watch him forcing his flaccid will into organized, energetic action as he pursues "Mrs. Havant" and, he believes, safety.

While neither Gary nor Kate turns out to be very likeable, both are vastly interesting people, and the war of will which takes place within each prepares the way for the war of wills between them. The struggle within and between protagonist and antagonist is echoed in the situations of minor characters. Kate's lover also confronts the problems revelation will create, and the victim's husband, Jeremy King, tries to balance his grief against his fury at the police who suspect him of the crime.

All these complications are very satisfying as are the convoluted chases featured prominently in the plot. Together, they make *The Point of Murder* satisfying reading, if not vintage Yorke. (Jane S. Bakerman)

Jane Langton. *The Memorial Hall Murder*. Harper & Row, 1978.

Fortuitously, we are supposed to believe, Homer Kelly, Jane Langton's out-sized detective of *The Transcendental Murder* (1964) and *Dark Nantucket Moon* (1975), is a visiting professor at Harvard when someone plants a bomb in Memorial Hall and the resulting explosion apparently kills Hamilton Dow, professor of music, cellist, and, at the time of the murder, director of rehearsals for a presentation of *The Messiah*. While Homer, the local, and the campus law search for Ham Dow's killer, the reader, who knows at once that the beloved conductor has survived the blast and is trapped in the wreckage below the disaster area, suffers considerable suspense wondering if the maestro will be rescued in time ... and also wondering about the identity of the corpse itself. Langton does a good job at concealing the identity of the murderer in this book; the clues are pretty fairly planted, but full revelation is nicely withheld until the conclusion.

Langton inserts alternate mini-chapters about Dow's survival techniques with the longer chapters which detail the investigation; every chapter begins with an unusual head note, a phrase--music and lyrics--of *The Messiah*. In fact, that selection becomes almost a character in the story, along with Memorial Hall itself. The music is intricate and lovely; the building is intricate and ugly, but both have enormous emotional overtones for the characters, and langton exploits both with great skill and success. Early on, she describes and characterizes the building:

> From the sidewalk on the other side of Kirkland Street, Homer Kelly looked solemnly at the sunless north facade of Memorial Hall. The building rose above him like a cliff face, mass piled upon mass, ten thousand of brick laid upon ten thousand. It was ugly. Majestically ugly. Augustly, monumentally ugly. It was a red-brick Notre Dame, a bastard Chartres, punctured with stained-glass windows, ribboned around with lofty sentiments in Latin, finialed with metallic crests and pennants, knobbed with the heads of orators, crowned with a bell tower and four giant clocks. Homer knew that the colossal edifice contained a theatre and a great hall and a memorial transept and a lecture room and a radio station and a lot of small offices and classrooms, but now in its gloomy grandeur it was a gigantic mausoleum as well. When it had been erected in the 1870s it had been intended as a half-secular, half-sacred memorial to young graduates who had died in the Union cause in the Civil War. Now it was an actual coffin.

Thus, Langton sets the tone of her story: suspense laced with a touch of horror (at Dow's potential fate). This tone is neatly undercut at well-chosen moments by humor and sentiment, qualities which arise from characterization.

As is her habit, Langton here again relies a bit too much on stereotypes, and these characters generate the humor. Chief among them are Julia Chamberlain, member of the Harvard Board of Overseers, and eccentric little Miss Plankton, peculiar member of the orchestra whose violin bow is always "rising steadfastly all by itself while the other bows descended." The sentiment is more deftly handled because it arises mostly from Vick Van Horn, "a thin, handsome girl with long hair pouring over her shoulders in a violent mass of red." Vick dearly loves Ham Dow, her teacher and mentor, and determines to complete the rehearsals and direct the performance of *The Messiah* as a proper memorial to the music master. Her grief and the stress she suffers as a neophyte conductor of this important and familiar work are very well rendered. Vick is a strong character and her presence and her efforts make a good sub plot.

In sum, *The Memorial Hall Murder* is a success; it's Langton at her best. (Jane S. Bakerman)

Jane Langton. *The Minuteman Murder*. Dell, 1980.

Jane Langton's *The Minuteman Murder* (originally published as *The Transcendental Murder* in 1964) is the fifty Murder Ink reprint in the current Dell series, and this introduction to Landton's continuing characters, Homer Kelly and Mary Morgan, is not only a worthy member of the series but also reasonably good fun in its own right. The plot revolves around the murder of Ernest Goss, an unlovable, cantankerous old meddler who claims to have uncovered heretofore unknown, scandalous love letters between such luminaries as Henry David Thoreau, Ralph Waldo Emerson, Margaret Fuller, and Louisa May Alcott. Goss intends to make a literary sensation by releasing the letters, a plan which alarms and irritates the members of the Alcott Association, worshippers all of Concord's nineteenth century circle of Transcendentalists. Because Ernest Goss is so unlovable, almost everyone we meet in contemporary Concord can be, and is, suspected of being the murderer.

Goss is killed in the midst of the Patriots' Day celebration which includes a parade and the reenactment of the less famous but completed ride of Dr. Samuel Prescott who spread the news in 1775 that the British were, indeed, coming. These events are followed by another ceremony; local citizens, in full costume and with authentic paraphernalia, commemorate the Battle of Concord while the Governor struggles to remember Long-fellow's poem which he intends to substitute for an original speech.

The governor's efforts are humorous, and, indeed, humor is the keynote of this novel. Much of that humor is centered around the sub plot, the awkward and halting courtship between Mary Morgan and Homer Kelly. Both hero and heroine are outsized people, a fact which Langton stretches too far in her efforts at being funny. Both, however, are extremely attractive poeple even though they are certainly not stereotypically handsome--and that fact is a big plus for the author. Both Mary and Homer are pursued by other suitors, and the reader is supposed to be breathless and intrigued by the question of whether or not they'll get together as clearly they should. *That* question actually doesn't generate one jot of suspense, but Langton's failure in this effort doesn't matter very much; the reader regrets her slump into triteness but reads on anyway. While Mary and Homer border on caricature, they are pretty well realized portraits; most of the other characters are extremely eccentric, however, and Langton capitalizes too much on New England stereotypes in creating them. Nevertheless, she sustains these characters pretty well, and they are fairly enjoyable.

Enormously enjoyable is the evocation of nineteenth century Concord, the reflection of the deep affection and awe in which dedicated students of the Transcendental period hold its major figures (an attitude worthy of the gentle fun which Langton pokes at it), and the aura of the little town itself, both then and now, is beautifully rendered. In fact, setting is probably the best asset of this very American transplanting of the English Country House Mystery. All in all, Jane Langton does a good piece of work in *The Minuteman Murder*; it's entertaining and pleasureful. (Jane S. Bakerman)

James McClure. *The Blood of an Englishman.* Harper & Row, 1980.

James McClure's Lieutenant Tromp Kramer and his aide, Detective Mickey Zondi, a Bantu, are back in action again in *The Blood of an Englishman*. McClure is in top form here; the action is brisk, and the characterizations are, as usual, excellent.

The excitement begins when the body of Bonzo Hookham, an English visitor to Trekkersburg, is found locked in the trunk of his sister's car. Eventually, the case is linked to a whole series of mysterious events in the white community. The final solution is not so much surprising as it is satisfying, but, nevertheless, the book is worthy of the series.

McClure has a sure hand with his plots, but some of the book's greatest interest lies in the folk who people it. Some are grotesque--for instance, the crew at the forensic lab. Some are appealing, such as Angela Kendall Westgate, friend of the victim. Westgate has reared her retarded son alone after her husband deserted her. Her control and courage, clearly shown but understated, reveal her grief over Hookham's death and the end of a warm relationship. Other minor characters are intriguing, such as Tish Hayes, a beautician who provides Kramer with a new love interest for this novel. If anyone cares--and Kramer certainly doesn't seem to--the Widow Fourie is out of town, at the beach for a holiday. Tish is likable, beautiful, passionate, clever, and fascinated with both Kramer and his work. Also, she is one of the few whites we have met who is decent to Zondi.

And, it is through Zondi, as usual, that McClure shines a clear and revealing light on the racism undergirding South African society. In this book again, as has often been the case in the past, Kramer must speak disparagingly of Zondi in order to protect Zondi's job and their relationship. Some of the social criticism comes in small details--Miriam Zondi, a careful housekeeper, scratches lines in the dirt floor of their shack to simulate a real floor. Other comments are more extended. The Zondi children have done well in school, and

their father wants to buy them a book as a reward. He must
submit to questioning by the white female clerk, pretend the
book is for his boss, and, finally, listen to her caution him
to "Carry it nicely, now" before he can get it off to himself
and savor the fine, new-book smell. Because readers, like
Kramer, know exactly how important Zondi is to the team's successful investigations, the irony is as effective as the comments are matter-of-fact.

McClure's narration is never shrill; social criticism
speeds rather than slows the plot, and he shows all aharacters
warts and all. He does a good job   (Jane S. Bakerman)

The Mystery Guild Anthology. Constable, 1980.

This is a collection of twelve new stories by writers who
have had books published by the Mystery Guild, one of Britain's
few mystery book clubs. The authors are Lovesey, Lord, Parrish (about Dan Mallett), Allbeury, Stuart, Celia Dale, Keating, Yorke, Doody (about Aristotle), Thomson, Cory and Brett.
A very even collection, and not one out-and-out loser. But
if I had to pick a favorite it would lie between Ted Allbeury's
spy story about "The Girl from Addis" and Lovesey's nasty
little opener which tells "How Mr. Smith Traced His Ancestors."
(Bob Adey)

Alan Sewart. *The Turn-Up.* Hale, 1978.

The main theme of this book is one of my favorites--the
digging up (in a redevelopment site in this case) of the skeleton of a murder victim of nearly forty years before. We then
follow the police team's efforts to establish the victim's
identity, and eventually the killer's. There's a fascinating
amount of detail included, and, while it may not quite come up
to such classics as Berkeley's *Murder in the Basement* and
Waugh's *A Rag and a Bone,* it is nevertheless a very competent
police procedural. (Bob Adey)

Audley Southcott. *Cross that Palm When I Come to It.* Sphere,
1974.

Novelization in episodic form of some of the early adventures (and misadventures) of seedy, down-at-the-heel private
detective Frank Marker, ITV's "Public Eye." The "Public Eye"
series ran intermittently for a number of years and, with
Alfred Burke as Marker, was way above average. Slightly offbeat, definitely low key. No heroics for Mr. Marker, and I
can't think why I didn't watch it more often. This book does
well to retain the flavour of the series as it takes the luck-
less Marker through the darkest days in his calling to what
might just be a light at the end of the tunnel. I believe
that there may have been a few more of these paperback
originals about Marker. I shall certainly look out for them.
(Bob Adey)

The Documents In the Case

(Letters)

From Charles MacDonald, 1533 Sperling Ave., Burnaby, B.C.:
While your flitting about is exhausting to cover, you are to be envied for your employability. Unless you enjoy packing, I hope that you stay with the horsies.
So damn glad you and Rex are to call it a day--or at least a year. BUT--what do you think of the TV mess. I hope that by next issue you will be fulminating. (I hope for so many things.) While William Conrad has not offended me (no more than most WC's), I think the programmes are done by people who have never read the books. While reading the books will cast doubt on the never-leave-the-house line, why did the series start on it? What a sentimental goop WC is. Who or what is Inspector Cramer--and those passionate glances from Archie to the gals?
Somebody should sue.
But keep up the good work--better you than so many.
[A recent article in TV Guide *speaks of the "meticulous research" that has gone into the production of the Nero Wolfe TV series, concluding that "Upon all of these efforts Wolfe would no doubt bestow his highest accolade: 'Most satisfactory.'" As one who has done a bit of meticulous research into the Nero Wolfe Saga, I feel no reluctance whatever to pronounce the article and its sentiments as being unsatisfactory in the extreme. I will not be drawn into a discussion of the travesty the TV series has made of Stout's stories and the characters that inhabit them--if I got started, the fifty pages of this issue would not be room enough to contain me--nor will I trust myself to comment on the physical aspects of the series beyond these few words--that if the yahoos in charge of Hollywood did not have it in their collective mind [sic] that any and all changes they choose to make in the works of masters are ipso facto improvements, they could have created a perfect facsimile of the brownstone for a fraction of the sum they expended on the cluttered, grossly inaccurate sets that forever offend the eye of the viewer who happens to be even marginally familiar with the original stories. As for what they've done to the stories, well.... We can, perhaps, console ourselves with the thought that, given the mentality that dominates the American television industry, it could have been worse--and probably will be. Next season, for example, we may be treated to a situation comedy based on* Crime and Punishment.*]*

From Helmuth Masser, Hermann Austgasse 3/25, A-8054 GRAZ, Aus-
tria/Oesterr.

I liked Bill Loeser's letter (TMF 5:1). It filled me with
enough rage to protest against what he has said about professors vs. amateurs in the field of writing about crime fiction.
And besides, answering his letter keeps me from preparing for
school without feelings of guilt.

I really don't know why Mr. Loeser should be so up against
those "professors." Is it because they have started to make a
livning from what amateurs have so far pursued with the purest
of hearts? Is it because they do know a lot about their stuff
and dare to let us have a look at their learning instead of
keeping their mouths shut? Or does Mr. Loeser fight those
poor professors because they use a kind of language that slightly differs from everyday English? Come, Mr. Loeser, do tell
me what you mean by "deadly." Are those professors too deadly
dull, too deadly serious, or even too deadly deep? Take this
Thompson guy with his Moral Visions, for example. His book,
which you prefer to call "such a thing," may have given a lot
of pleasure to Hammett fans, and it certainly did to me. Whether Thompson is right or wrong in his views is of little im-
portance to the fan. What matters is the way in which he pre-
sents his opinions; and what he has to say about the Op in Red
Harvest or Beaumont in The Glass Key betrays a lot of insight
into man's nature, an insight which I for one didn't have.
Anyway, the book gives me and I'm sure others as well more information than mere charts, diagrams, lists of characters and
the like (however valuable they are, mind you!).

You've referred to Cawelti's gook as an exception to the
rule that most professional writing is "deadly." Good God--he
is by no means what some would call an "easy read." In my
opinion, the only difference between a Thompson and a Cawelti
is that the latter is much harder to read, or more "deadly"
serious. What's so bad about looking at Hammett from a Marx-
ist's point of view, for example? Or any other point of view?
Crime writers and their work are by no means sacrosanct, something to be put in shrines; they should be discussed, analyzed,
torn apart, put together again, but not protected from poison-
ous views or simply worshipped like the ones that have already
been canonized by time (or the Queen cousins).

I'm fully aware that a lot of analytical material is rub-
bish--whether it has been done by professors or living amateurs; looking at my bookshelves I could easily point out the
few that gave me real pleasure (insight + good style) and the
legions that let me down, people that mromised me a lot and
kept little or nothing, but charged me all the same.

I'm not going to raise outcries from among readers and
contributors to TMF by giving names (coward me)--I'd hate being kicked from TMF's subscription list [no chance of that] as
an unworthy pagan--but to me some of the holy scriptures of
mystery fandom seem pretty earthly.

As there's no amateur writing done in Austria and little
in Germany, most of the diet is supplied by German "academia";
and the name Cawelti in Mr. Loeser's letter has reminded me of
a book by Ranier Burkhardt (Die "hartgesottene" Amerikanische
Detektivgeschichte und ihre gesellschaftliche Funktion, Frank-
fort, 1978). Sounded interesting enough and yet gave me the
shock of my life. I had wrongly expected a history of the
genre but had got a book with an emphasis on the psyche of the

compulsive reader of hardboiled stuff (the loving fan, so to say) and on the social and economic conditions in America that brought about hardboiled literature. If anyone had asked me then what I thought of the book I would have strongly advised him to keep off it. And for quite some time I lost all interest in crime fiction. I know how frustrating and joy killing analytical material can be--but on the other hand it was the wrong book for the wrong person at the wrong time. Rereading it--much slower this time--together with more thinking on my part opened a book to me which I hadn't done justice to at first.

And the same may be said of a lot of amateur writing in the field. Take a review of a long-forgotten Daly book in TMF, for example. It doesn't look precious enough to file, and yet the proud owner of the book has put all his love of Daly in his short review and slowly you realize that you won't find better information elsewhere. So what? Well, from my experience I can say: vivant professores (but only those who aren't phoneys) and long life to the amateurs (who are both loving *and* interesting and not after my money with a shoddy book...).

Well, Mr. Townsend, take it or leave it, it was fun to write this letter. [*It was fun to read it, too, but what's with all these "Mr.'s"? If there's one thing I've striven for in these pages it's informality. In fact, some might say that my success along those lines has far exceeded their hopes or expectations ...*]

From Bill Crider, 4206 Ninth St., Brownwood, TX 76801:

It was only after reading Jane Gottschalk's letter in the latest TMF that I realized how much John Nieminski looks like Archie Goodwin. Not quite as much like Archie as I do, but there is a definite resemblance. Of course it's true that John and I do look a great deal alike, but what most people don't know is that we also write alike and that as a matter of fact I've been writing most of John's stuff for several years now. Keep this under your hat, please.

Martin Wooster's review of 20thCC&MW leaves me wondering just what category I belong in. I'm afraid to reread any of my essays for fear that I'll be the enthusiastic fan or the dreaded academic. Unfortunately, there's no way that I can be classified with the patriotic professionals. Aside from my own fears, though, I think Martin has a point. I'd disagree, though, that Bill Pronzini's articles on "relatively obscure" writers constitutes anything like "extensive analysis." Besides, I would think that one of the values of a book like 20thCC&MW would be that it does provide information on these very writers, information that is available nowhere else.

This far along in the season, I've developed some more opinions on the Wolfe TV show. I'd say the series is in deep trouble, all right, but mainly because the writers have now tried to humanize Wolfe too much. In last week's version of *Murder by the Book*, Wolfe was behaving like a big teddy bear by the show's end. Not only did he allow the girl to give him a peck on the cheek, he looked as if he enjoyed it. And his little "thumb's up" signal to Archie at the end was the last straw. Too, my worst fears about *Magnum P.I.* have become reality. Last week, Magnum turned and mugged for the camera;

his identification with Burt Reynolds has become complete.

I was as glad as everyone else to have Steve Lewis back, and the letters were entertaining. I hope the trend in letter writing continues.

From Bob Briney, 4 Forest Ave., Salem, MA 01970:

It looks as if I will never have any more "free" time than I do now (as I should have been able to foresee), so I might as well get this short and inadequate letter in response to recent TMFs.

It is a relief to learn that the readers' response was so positive and that the magazine will continue. I'm sorry that the Postal Service gobbled my copy of 4:5, so I couldn't join in the response. The replacement was eminently worth waiting for, full of information and informed opinion. As always, Steve Lewis's reviews are a major attraction.

In 4:6, Ev Bleiler refers to the "U. of Ca. sponsorship of TAD." In actual fact, there never was any such thing. While the California air did eventually prove to be unhealthy for the magazine, the University was not involved. TAD was not part of The Mystery Library (in spite of some publicity to the contrary) and was handled by Publisher's Inc. independently of their dealings with the University. If TAD *had* fallen under University sponsorship, it would have suffered far more than it did from the sojourn in sunny climes.

Re: the jigsaw puzzle stories which Robert Samoian mentions: the Clayton Rawson story at least is in print. It was reprinted in EQMM, August 1961, as "Merlini and the Photographic Clues," and is included in the book *The Great Merlini*, Gregg Press, 1979.

[*Later* ...]

A slightly tardy letter on TMF 5:1. The new cover layout, the well-designed column-headings (who gets the credit for them? [*your not-so-humble editor, that's who*]), and the spot illustrations (ditto [*ditto*]) give the magazine a tidy, well-organized, and settled look which is very pleasing. One can easily envision a long row of such issues on the shelf.... I agree with Bob Napier, however, that varying the vignette on the cover would liven things up a bit.

I have enjoyed Barry Van Tilburg's dossiers on "spy series characters," but I hope no other entry in the series has suffered the same fate as the current one on Nayland Smith: somewhere along the line, the biographical and bibliographical facts have become rather thoroughly fouled up. To begin with, Van Tilburg never mentions Smith's title, although for most of his chronicled career (eleven out of fourteen books) Smith is *Sir* Denis Nayland Smith. (He picks up the "Sir" and the "Denis" at the same time, as a matter of fact; in the first three books he is just plain Nayland Smith.)

The dossier says "Starts the series as a Chief Superintendent and when war breaks out works for British Intelligence." The facts are approximately the opposite. Early in the first book, Smith describes himself as "a servant of the British Government, lately stationed in Burma" and says, "I have got a roving commission." The action of the book makes it clear that Smith is not at this time connected with Scotland Yard, though he does possess a mysterious warrant card which enables him to commandeer police services at will. After a gap of thirteen years between book #3 and book #4, Smith reappears

as Sir Denis Nayland Smith, Assistant Commissioner of Scotland
Yard. At no time is the rank of Chief Superintendent mentioned,
nor is there any mention in the series of "the war," either I
or II. Much later, after World War II, Smith reverts to his
roving Intelligence work; in *Shadow of Fu Manchu* he is referred
to as "ex-chief of the Criminal Investigation Department of
Scotland Yard." "He was in New York at the request of the
Federal Bureau of Investigation, and had been given almost
autocratic powers by Washington."
       Among "associates" a certain Kerrigan is listed. Bart
Kerrigan is the narrator of two of the books, *The Drums of Fu
Manchu* and *The Island of Fu Manchu*. He is no more nor less
worthy of being singled out as a Smith associate than Shan
Greville (*Daughter* and *Mask*) or Alan Sterling (*Bride* and *Trail*).
Inspector Weymouth and Sir Lionel Barton are present in four
or more of the books, and are certainly worth mentioning.
       "Nigel Green and Peter Sellers have portrayed Smith in the
movies." So have Fred Paul (1923-24), O.P. Heggie (1929-30),
Lewis Stone (1932), William Royel (1940), Douglas Wilmer (1966-
67), Richard Greene (1969); and on TV, Sir Cedric Hardwicke
(1950) and Lester Matthews (1956).
       In the checklist of Fu Manchu books (well, they are cer-
tainly not Nayland Smith books!), Van Tilburg seems to have
got *Collier's* magazine confused with the P.F. Collier Co. Most
of the Fu stories originally appeared in *Collier's*-the-magazine,
and the first nine or ten of them were included in a matched
set of hardcover reprints ("The Orient Edition") issued by the
Collier Co. These reprints usually used the original hardcover plates, but they did not appear until long after the
first editions. Thus all of the references to "Collier" in
the checklist should be deleted. The alternative titles for
the first three books are British titles; the books never appeared in the U.S. under those titles. *Daughter of Fu Manchu*
was never published by McBride; it was issued by Doubleday,
Doran. And there is no *The* in the title. I have never heard
of anything called *The Fu Manchu Book*. There was a book
called *The Book of Fu Manchu,* an omnibus collection of earlier
novels, published by McBride in 1929 (and by Hurst & Blackett
in England in the same year).
       Phew! I don't know how much (if anything) of the preced-
ing you will feel like printing, but in justice to good old
Nayland (not to mention Fu) I thought the facts should be set
straight.
       E.F. Bleiler's solid scholarship is as satisfying as usual,
and he does the service of warning us away from a book that
might otherwise have been tempting. I have only recently seen
(for the third time) the Sondheim/Wheeler version of *Sweeney
Tod,* with Angela Lansbury; fascinating theatre! ## An interesting subject for inquiry would be the use of Sweeney Todd
in mystery fiction. There is, for example, a brief play (probably an adaptation of a radio play) by John Dickson Carr called
"Flight from Fleet Street," whose main action takes place in
a Fleet Street barber shop operated by a certain Henry S.
Todd ....
       Though Marv Lachman's column and Steve Lewis's reviews are
as enjoyable as always, the twenty pages of letters are the
high point of this issue. Reading them is like being at a
party with a bunch of enthusiastic and knowledgeable people
and miraculously being able to hear all the conversations go-

ing on.... Including that squint-eyed, red-headed fellow who
sits in the corner muttering in parentheses.

From Iwan Hedman, Flodins väg 5, 152 00 Strängnäs, Sweden:
     Congratulations on your new--permanent, I hope--address.
I can't understand how you can stand it moving like you have
done so many times. I am fortunate enough not having moved
from our house since 1959. Of course, I can't think about
moving about 20,000 books from one place to another ....
     Have just got your excellent issue TMF No 1/Jan 1981, have
just read it, and I feel I must write a few lines to your letter section, which I find one of the most readable things in
TMF. Of course you also have a lot of fine articles, but I
think I get so much out of reading all those letters from
people I know--though I have not met them in person, except
for a few of them. Still, they are familiar to me, names such
as John Nieminsky, Charles Shibuk, Marv Lachman, Bob Adey, Jon
Breen, Ev Bleiler, David Doerrer (a close pen-pal since some
back issues of TMF), and all the others. Going from first to
last page of this issue I'll start at the beginning. Barry
Van Tilburg's series about the Spy Series Characters in Hard-
back is an excellent one, and I have also got permission to
run some of them in my own DAST (will of course rewrite part
of it for Swedish readers). I did also like the article about
Tony Hillerman, who has one or two books translated into
Swedish.
     I can also agree with what Martin M. Wooster is saying
about the "Bible," *Twentieth-Century Crime and Mystery Writers*.
Still I must say that book is one of the best published in our
genre. In such a big work you can always find some items
which are not as good as others.
     Looking forward to Jon Breen's coming book *What About
Murder?* from the Scarecrow Press.
     This issue looks like a great tribute to the latest Boucher-
con--although some reproduced pictures seem to have been a bit
odd, adding fifty years of age to some people--making some
people look like old mummies (Wenstrup's letter was very funny,
I think).
     When reading about that Pocket Book Price Guide I think I
must ask you readers of TMF something: in my own DAST-MAGAZINE
I have some booklists each time it is published. Some of
these books are sometimes very hard to find and therefore I
have decided to have auctions on them. That means you have a
deadline for your bid. I do that because the postal service
(wrong word, they don't have any service at all today) makes
DAST arrive at subscribers on different days, even if I send
it out on the same day. What do you think of the method of
having an auction? I think it's a better chance for everyone
to get the book he/she wants?
     Also looking forward to Al Hubin's new edition of his Bib-
liography. I think his new idea to put two new sections in
that book is good, especially the one about including biographical information about the authors. I've done that in my
Bibliography of all books published in the Swedish language
and all the buyers of my book are satisfied with that.
     I am working on a new edition of my book, too, and I also
hope to have it ready for publication in 1982 (500 pages and
about 500 illustrations). Yesterday night I talked to Harald
Mogensen (the Danish collector) and he told me that he and

Tage la Cour are working on a new edition of their book, *Mord-bogen*.

I can agree in what you are saying about that CBS interview with Otto Penzler. If you *only* show the viewers those very very odd and expensive items, they can lose interest in collecting. They know they can never get enough money to buy such an item. Instead, if you show them some ordinary items you could make them feel they can make it, too.

Yes, Myrtis Broset, it's absolutely too much sex and violence in books today. Let me tell you a short story about that. My wife had read thrillers and mysteries for a long time and suddenly she got sick of all that speculative sex and violence in them so she told me that she was changing from those books to a book by one of the best Swedish authors who happened to be a member of the Swedish Academy (writing only good fiction), but to her horror and great surprise she found that book more filled with sex than the other. She was almost shocked.

If my friend Elmore Mundell can't find a copy of the University of Texas guide to that Queen Collection, I do have a copy he can borrow.

To Bill Loeser I can add that the best book about butterflies is still the one made by an amateur. Amateurs are almost doing better jobs in their own field than professionals-- and that is specially when doing bibliographies.

From Otto Penzler, 129 West 56th St., New York, NY 10019:
Bless Becky Reineke's heart. The show that I did with Ray Brady on CBS had little to do with what was actually filmed. The crew and Brady were at The Mysterious Bookshop for about three hours' worth of filming, which was then edited down to the four or five minutes that aired. *I* sure don't get up at that hour of the day, so I didn't see it, but I know that only the Big Names were used and the *only* topic of conversation was the Big Bucks that each of the books was worth. Yes, the figures I gave are accurate, but I hate that sort of thing as much as anybody. I've been collecting for about twenty years now and never got into it, as the vernacular goes, for the great financial killing to be reaped. Who knew? I'm a full-time bookseller now, so I have to deal in prices and values and dollars and all that, but none of us with the infection can ever defend or explain the hobby (Passion) to those who don't share it. Finding a dust-jacketed copy of an obscure turn-of-the-century mystery is more exciting than finding a dust-jacketed Hammett or Chandler, though the "value" is far less. So What? We do it because we love it, and we'll never be able to make the philistines understand. Don't bother to try to defend your hobby, Becky. Remember that there are people--millions of them--who prefer formica to mahogany, Andy Warhol to Claude Lorraine, and The Rolling Stones to Mozart.

From Pauline W. Osborn, The Book Rack, Bonanza Mini-Mall, Starkville, MS 39759:
Can you find me *Hamlet, Revenge!* by Michael Innes? [*Anyone?*]

From John M. Reilly, 293 Washington Ave., Albany, NY 12206:
I wonder if you would permit me to use "The Documents in the Case" to announce an error in *Twentieth Century Crime and*

Mystery Writers?

The entry for Alistair MacLean includes several books actually written by Ian Stuart. The reason for this mistake is that MacLean, early in his career, used the pseudonym Ian Stuart for two books (*The Dark Crusader*, published as *The Black Shrike* in the U.S., and *The Satan Bug*). Later works published under that name by the *real* Ian Stuart have become linked to the MacLean name in several reference sources, library catalogs, and book indexes. The fact that Alistair MacLean's middle name is Stuart does not help, either. The real Ian Stuart deserves independent critical assessment, and I regret having hindered that. For the record, readers ought to know that Stuart's novels are: *The Snow on the Ben* (Ward Lock, 1961), *Death from Disclosure* (Robert Hale, 1976), *Flood Tide* (Hale, 1977), *Sand Trap* (Hale, 1977), *Fatal Switch* (Hale, 1978), *A Weekend to Kill* (Hale, 1978), *Pictures in the Dark* (Hale, 1979), *The Renshaw Strike* (Hale, 1980), and *End on the Rocks* (forthcoming from Hale, 1981). Mr. Ian Stuart has also written numerous short stories and serials. It is possible that some of his works will appear in U.S. editions soon, so I am especially sorry about the error. I offer apologies to Mr. Stuart, Mr. MacLean, and to readers of *Twentieth Century Crime and Mystery Writers*.

From Joh Breen, 10642 La Bahia Ave., Fountain Valle, CA 92708:

What About Murder?, an unjacketed volume of about 150 pages, will sell for a mere $10! Your readers who wish to avail themselves of this amazing bargain may write to Scarecrow Press, 52 Liberty Street, P.O. Box 656, Metuchen, NJ 08840. It should be published in April so will probably be available by the time your next issue aypears. The same firm has contracted to publish a collection of my mystery parodies in 1982. (If anyone has a snappy title for such a collection, I can't offer a cut in the royalties but will provide an acknowledgement in the book.)

To Linda Toole: It was Phyllis Kirk, not Newman, who played Nora to Peter Lawford's Nick in the TV version of *The Thin Man*.

Al Hubin's letter re the Edgars troubles me. Does Harper and Row's failure to submit nominees mean that Margaret Doody's *Aristotle Detective* and Leonard Tourney's *The Player's Boy Is Dead* will *not* be considered for best first novel? In other words, does the commettee feel bound to consider only those titles submitted by their publishers? I am currently serving on the paperback Edgar committee. Here, too, publishers are invited to nominate titles--and, in fact, all of the top contenders have been nominated in that way--but members of the committee are encouraged to watch out for good paperback originals that have not been nominated by their publishers.

Saw the Nero Wolfe TV show's version of *In the Best Families* last night. It was not a bad job, though obviously some aspects of the book could not be done on TV and the circumstances of Wolfe's going under cover had to be changed somewhat. The plot (and the main clue, one of Stout's better ones) seemed to be kept approximately intact. The main trouble with the series is that Conrad does much too energetic a Wolfe--one could imagine this Wolfe browbeating Archie to get to work instead of the reverse. Generally I don't think the casting is bad at all. Lee Horsley is an adequate Archie, though not an ideal one, and Conrad is a respectable Wolfe who would be even better if he'd quit bouncing around so much. Admittedly, Cramer is far from the character in the books and Saul Panzer has been badly done by. But with good scripts, the present cast would be okay.

As I read Bob Adey's letter, he means an Englishman would *not* refer to walking two blocks. The phrase "an American Holmes story" means a Holmes story set in England but written by an American, not a Holmes story set in America. My English wife agrees that a Briton would refer to a distance walked in terms of time or miles, since the term block means nothing in a country where the cities are generally not laid out in blocks as they are here.

The bibliography from Greenwood Press, *Crime, Detective, Espionage, Mystery and Thriller Fiction and Film*, lists a lot of good stuff, but its usefulness is limited by its lack of annotations. Also, it omits material from fanzines, even limiting TAD references to those that have been listed in other secondary sources. Garland is coming out with a volume called *Crime Fiction Criticism*, edited by Timothy and Julia Johnson, which will be annotated and will include articles from TAD, though not (I think) other fanzines. I haven't seen it yet, but it will probably be available by the time this issue appears. I'd wait to find out about the Garland entry before acquiring the Greenwood. [*I read the Garland book in typescript last year. It is certainly a useful source, but it has its limitations. An indication of how comprehensive it is can be seen in the fact that only about twenty of the 112 critical pieces on Stout which are identified in our recent Stout bibliography are cited in the Johnson book. If that holds for all authors, it means that the Johnsons managed to run down only about one in five or six of the critical works extant. One problem, as Jon suggests, is that the Johnsons ignored all fanzines except TAD, and approached the problem more or less from the point of view that if an item was not likely to be available in a major university library it didn't deserve mention. I offered to make many sources available to the Johnsons, including runs of fanzines other than TAD, but my offer was never acknowledged, much less accepted. Still, it's a useful work, and probably worth the no doubt outrageous price that Garland will be asking for it.*]

From Bob Aucott, 28 W. Waverly Road, Glenside, PA 19038:

I'm considerably puzzled by parts of Martin Morse Wooster's "discussion" in TMF 5:1 of *Twentieth-Century Crime and Mystery Writers*, and unless somebody can help me, or until I've read more of the book, perhaps (I've skipped a lot of writers I'm not much interested in), I'll probably stay puzzled. "Half of this volume," says Mr. Wooster, "is brilliant, and half is quite bad." Maybe he's sort of rounding off the percentages, but that statement seems to indicate that the book contains an awful lot of waste space. Have I read only the good half?

I can follow him as he divides into *tres partes*, etc., the world of mystery criticism, and I share his high opinion of the "solid appreciations" of, for example, Messrs. Briney, Nevins and Shibuk, three of my favorite critics/fans. I can sympathize, too, with his belief that many writers are probably over-analyzed--too obscure for most of us--but they *do* belong in the book, and are generally most intelligently discussed by Bill Pronzini and others (my only criticism of Bill's contributions, by the way, is of his rating of the Geoffrey Homes books; this is chiefly because Bill doesn't mention *my* favorite, *Then There Were Three*, a unique classic, I think).

And finally, I agree, to a great extent, with Mr. Wooster's dislike of the pedantry of many of his "academics."

But, suddenly, he loses me. Not only does he seem a bit unfair to Robert Parker--surely really a "professional," and a brilliant one--but in identifying Joann Harack Hayne as the worst of the pedants, and in singling out her essay on Peter Lovesey as the absolute nadir, Mr. Wooster seems to me so absurdly wrong as to make me suspicious, almost, of *all* his judgements.

Ms. Hayne's essay on Lovesey, *according to Mr. Wooster*, refers to Sergeant Cribb's creator as having "written dismal tomes," as "predictable," as having "deliberately set out to produce a universe of lifeless drones." In so doing, she has apparently incurred Mr. Wooster's considerable displeasure. Are Mr. Wooster and I reading the same essay? Are we even in the same book? I had read the Lovesey write up: I read it again.

Ms. Hayne accuses Lovesey of *none* of these things. Her essay is almost entirely favorable to him, and very much so. And she gives good reasons. Some of her judgements are: an "always firm grasp of historical details"; usually ingenious"; "a compensating ... undercurrent of humour"; a "wise ... lightness of tone"; "amusingly original plots'; "fascinating tidbits of Victoriana"; "skillful use of quotations." Her lone unfavorable remark is that "a spark of life or fantasy ... is missing from some of the Lovesey books." Not too horrid, is it? Pedantic? Prolix and fatuous, as Mr. Wooster says? Surely not.

Why has Ms. Hayne received Mr. Wooster's condemnation? I am baffled, and I am disappointed in him. He gives her no good marks for her other essays, either, all of which seemed to me sympathetic and perceptive. Can it bee that in Mr. Wooster we have a critic in whom the neap tide of the milk of human kindness is not at its height? Should I *not* be puzzled? Is it I who am confused. Or is it Mr. Wooster?

Enough. Oh, one more thing. I can't go along with Marvelous Marv's Third Law entirely, though I sympathize. How about *The Dain Curse*? *The China Roundabout* (Josephine Bell)? *The Bletchington Tangle* (G.D.H. and M.I. Cole)? *The Dangerfield Talisman* and *The Castleford Conundrum* (both J.J. Connington)? *The Catalyst Club*? *The Judas Window*? *The Megstone Plot*? *The Massingham Affair*? *The Bellamy Trial*? *The Congo Venus*? *The Appleby File*? *The Spanish Steps*? *The Hammersmith Maggot*? Surely, it's a time honored and not an uncommon device. I think Mr. Lachman (one of our great scholars in the field) should restate Law Three. Perhaps it should apply only to *recent* titles? (The Dallas Green, The Pete Rose, The John Bench, The Mickey Mantle.)

From Mike Cook, 3318 Wimberg Ave., Evansville, IN 47712:
I am in the finishing stages of a book, *Monthly Murders*, that will list in chronological order all of the fiction contents of all the U.S. and British digest-size mystery magazines, serve as a checklist, and include also a composite

author's index along with other features. The book has been
accepted for publication by Greenwood Press.
However, I am in urgent need of the more elusive magazines,
and would like to locate collectors who may have some of them
and would supply me with the contents information. I would be
glad to pay for this, including photocopying of the contents
pages, or just the information. I would be glad to send a
list of the specific issues I am lacking, and would refund
postage also. Among those magazines of which I am missing
some: *Bestseller Mystery Magazine, Double-Action, Detective
Fiction, Ed McBain, Executioner, Fast-Action, Guilty, Homicide,
Hunted, Keyhole, Killers, Malcolms, Mystery Digest, Manhunt
(12/63 only), Mercury Mystery Magazine, Mysterious Traveler,
Nero Wolfe, Offbeat, Pocket Detective, Pursuit, Surefire,
Shock, Suspect, Web, Terror, Tightrope, Trapped, Two-Fisted,*
and *Verdict.*

From Louise Gagnon, 8-308 Blake Blvd., Vanier, Ontario, Canada:
A few days ago I received eighteen back issues of TMF and
had to stop in the midst of a positive orgy of reading pleasure to say that if what I haven't read lives up to my expectations you've found another lifetime subscriber.
A few years ago I began subscribing to TAD as a result of
a mention in a local newspaper column dealing with specialist
periodicals. It was something of a shock to realize that
there were many people out there with similar interests. I
never thought of myself as a collector since I only keep those
books I am going to want to reread, but letters from readers
looking for titles I had been hoarding for years (e.g., Richard Stark, Ed McBain, Rex Stout) convinced me that I qualified
at least in a minor way.
In spite of this, I never attempted to write to TAD. This
was partly because the slickness of the publication and "PhD"-
type articles seemed out of my league, and also because my refusal to pay first-class postage means that I usually receive
my copy much too late to comment on anything within a reasonable length of time. However, your homey format and the
friendliness of your contributors all seem to be saying, "Come
on in, the water's fine."
So far, I have been reading only "Mysteriously Speaking"
and "The Documents in the Case," but judging by the comments
in the letters I have many pleasant surprises in store. I am
looking forward to reading the reviews, especially those by
Stephen Lewis, but I am saving up the best for this weekend.
At least once a year on a cold, wet February weekend, or,
let's be honest, even a sunny July weekend, in fact anytime I
can put together an uninterrupted stretch of time, I get out
all my Nero Wolfes, start at the beginning and work my way
through. This weekend, however (since I have one of those
stretches of time coming up, your timing could not have been
better), I intend to read the Wolfe saga Parts V to XIX--
ecstacy indeed.
Although I have been immersed in TMF since it arrived I
did take time out to watch "Rumpole of the Bailey" on PBS.
Although the mystery elements are minor, I am thoroughly en-
joying this view into what "barristers" really do in "cham-
bers." When I reread some of my favourite (excuse the British
spelling, but we Canadians are funny that way) British legal
mysteries, I will look at them in a different, or at least a

more familiar way.

While on the subject of television mysteries, I wonder what your opinion is of the Nero Wolfe series starring William Conrad. While I feel that almost any NW is better than none, I am only slowly adjusting to the fact that none of the recurring characters, or objects, for that matter (e.g., the globe), look the way they have in my head for many years.

Something which happened over the past weekend has led me to believe (hope, aspire) that I may be able to contribute to TMF in the future. In both NYTBR and *Time* I read reviews of a mystery novel entitled *A Treasure Alarm* by Jocelyn Davey. I gather that it has just been published by Walker in the United States. A glance at our library copy indicates that we have had the British edition since February of 1977. Although this is an extreme example, it is true that a) living in Canada and b) working in a library, I often have access to British mysteries, e.g. Dick Francis, a year or two before they are available in the U.S. When I surface from eighteen TMF's at one shot, I would like to attempt to review some of these. [*Do, by all means.*]

From Linda Toole, 147 Somershire Dr., Rochester, NY 14617:

Since my last letter, John McAleer has assured me that you do exist, he has met you, and, in his words, you "are a handsome young fellow in his early thirties, rather the Audie Murphy type in appearance." [*Audie Murphy? Handsome? Audie Murphy?? Early thirties? Audie Murphy???*]

To complete my reply to Frank Floyd, I have now seen three episodes of Nero Wolfe on TV and all-in-all I'm reacting rather favorably. Cramer is badly miscast, the Horstmann-Wolfe interplay rings false (if not downright insubordinate), and Fritz's part is much too small. The house is gorgeous (of course there are things wrong with it, but all-in-all ...) and Horsley has promise as Archie--much better than I thought at first. Conrad moves about too much, but I'm afraid that's due to television and can't be helped. I'm really rather satisfied with him, and don't mind the beard at all! One minor point of genius was the casting of Johnny Keems in *Might as Well Be Dead*--just slightly sleazy. Purley Stebbins is also good. I'm sure that many, many people will disagree with me--from mildly to violently--but, as I said before, I don't really expect perfection from TV, and I am relatively happy when things are better than mediocre. Since this is TMF and not *The Gazette*, I'll limit my comments. Perhaps future locs will warrant another letter on this topic.

Does the proposed postage increase affect other classes of mail--specifically your permit? [*Of course.*]

From Mike Nevins, 7045 Cornell, University City, MO 63130:

Thanks for another fine issue of TMF. It seems that God doesn't want me to write you that article on the Nero Wolfe TV series, because for the last several Friday evenings I've had to be away from my set....

As you may have heard, Robert L. Fish died of a heart attack a couple of weeks ago. He was not only one of the most active members of MWA but one of those whom it was pure and simple fun to be with, and as much as we'll all miss the novels he would have written, we'll miss Bob himself even more.